Dick King-Smith

Ace
and
Noah's Brother

Illustrated by Liz Graham-Yooll
and Ian Newsham

PUFFIN BOOKS

Published by the Penguin Group
Penguin Books Ltd, 27 Wrights Lane, London W8 5TZ, England
Penguin Books USA Inc., 375 Hudson Street, New York, New York 10014, USA
Penguin Books Australia Ltd, Ringwood, Victoria, Australia
Penguin Books Canada Ltd, 10 Alcorn Avenue, Toronto, Ontario, Canada M4V 3B2
Penguin Books (NZ) Ltd, 182–190 Wairau Road, Auckland 10, New Zealand

Penguin Books Ltd, Registered Offices: Harmondsworth, Middlesex, England

Ace first published by Victor Gollancz Ltd 1990
Published in Puffin Books 1991
Noah's Brother first published by Victor Gollancz Ltd 1986
Published in Puffin Books 1988
A Puffin Book exclusively for School Book Fairs 1994
1 3 5 7 9 10 8 6 4 2

Filmset in Bembo

Printed in England by Clays Ltd, St Ives plc

Ace

Dick King-Smith

Illustrated by
Liz Graham-Yooll

Contents

Ace

CHAPTER I

A Pig with a Mark

"Well I never! Did you ever?" said Farmer Tubbs.

He was leaning on the wall of his pigsty, looking down at a sow and her litter of piglets. The sow was asleep, lying on her side, and six of her seven piglets slept also, their heads pillowed on their mother's huge belly.

But the seventh piglet was wide awake, and stood directly below the farmer, ears cocked, staring up at the man with bright eyes that had in them a look of great intelligence.

"I never seed one like you afore," said Farmer Tubbs. "Matter of fact, I don't suppose there's ever been one like you, eh?"

In reply the piglet gave a single grunt. Farmer Tubbs was not a fanciful man, but he did, just for a moment, fancy that the grunt sounded more like a 'No' than an 'Oink'. He half expected the piglet to shake its head.

A Pig with a Mark

Up till that time he had not noticed anything out of the ordinary about this litter. But what was now catching his attention was the seventh piglet's strange marking, clearly to be seen once he was standing apart from his brothers and sisters. On his left side there was an oddly-shaped black spot.

The sow was a mongrel, numbering amongst her ancestors Large Whites, Saddlebacks and Gloucester Old Spots. Usually her piglets were white with bluish patches, but occasionally a baby would be born with the odd spot or two on it, so it was not remarkable that this piglet should have one. What was however extremely unusual was the formation of the single black marking. It stood out clearly against a white background, and it was almost exactly the shape of the symbol that stands for a club in a pack of playing-cards.

"Will you look at that!" said Farmer Tubbs. "It's a club, a single one! And a card with a single marking is called an ace, young feller-me-lad, d'you know that?"

In answer the piglet gave two quick grunts. Somehow they sounded different from the 'No' grunt, sharp, impatient, almost like 'Yes, Yes'.

"Fancy!" said Farmer Tubbs. "I wonder you never nodded at me."

He scratched with the point of his stick at the black

marking on the piglet's side.

"There be no doubt," he said, "what us shall have to call you. I don't never give names to piglets as a rule—they don't live long enough to make no odds—but us shall have to name you."

The piglet stood silent and motionless, apparently noting every word that was said.

"Your name," said Farmer Tubbs, "is written on you. The Ace of Clubs, that's who you be."

For some while longer the farmer stood leaning on the pigsty wall, chatting to the piglet. Farmer Tubbs enjoyed a nice chat, and since he lived alone and saw few other people, he spent a good deal of time talking either to himself or to his animals.

"If things had turned out different," he said now to the newly-named Ace of Clubs, "and I'd married when I were a young man, I'd likely have had six or seven children by now like your mum has. But I can't say as I'm sorry. Maybe it'd have been nice to have a wife to chat to, but you can have too much of a good thing. Only girl I ever fancied marrying, she were a good strong wench and she were a wonderful cook but, my, didn't she go on! Talk the hind leg off a donkey, she could, you couldn't never have a proper conversation with she, you wouldn't get a word in edgeways. We was engaged for a bit, but then she broke it off and went and wed a sheep farmer, long thin fellow name of Hogget. And I'll tell you a funny thing, young Ace of Clubs, are you listening?"

The piglet grunted twice.

"As well as sheep, Hogget had a pig, a huge old white boar, and that boar could round up sheep, just like a dog. You wouldn't never think that were possible, would you?"

The piglet grunted once.

"Well, 'tis true," said Farmer Tubbs, "and what's more, now I comes to think of it, that clever old boar was your great-grandfather! So you never knows, young Ace—you might be an extrahordinary pig when you'm full-grown."

Except you never will be full-grown, thought the farmer. I shall sell you and your brothers and sisters when you'm eight weeks old, and a few months after that you'll all be pork.

He was careful only to think all this and not to say it out loud. Why, he asked himself? Well, the piglet might understand what he was saying, this one might.

Farmer Tubbs's fat red face creased into a great smile and he shook his head and tapped his forehead with one finger.

"You'm daft, Ted Tubbs, you are!" he cried. "Who ever heard of a pig that could understand the Queen's

ACE

English! Can you imagine such a thing, Ace, eh, can you?"

The piglet grunted twice.

CHAPTER 2

A Pig with a Gift

"Mother?" said the Ace of Clubs one morning, six or seven weeks later.

"Yes, dear?"

"What's that noise outside the sty?"

"It's the farmer's pick-up truck, dear."

"What's he going to pick up, Mother?"

"You, dear. You and your brothers and sisters. To take you for a nice ride."

"Where to, Mother?"

Though the sow knew the correct answer to this question, she did not actually understand what it meant. Over the years, all her children had disappeared to this destination at a certain age, and, to be frank, she was always quite glad to see them go. Raising a litter of ever-hungry piglets was *so* demanding.

"You're going to Market," she said comfortably.

"Where's that?"

"It's a place," said the sow, "a very popular place for a holiday I should imagine, judging by the number of animals of all sorts that go to Market. You'll like it there. You'll make lots of new friends, I expect, and have a lovely time."

Ace's six brothers and sisters grew very excited at these words, and ran round the sty squealing. But Ace stood still and looked thoughtful.

"But Mother," he said. "Why do we have to go to Market? I like it here. I don't want to go. Why must I?"

"Why must you ask so many questions?" said the sow sharply, and she went into the inner part of the sty and flopped down in the straw with a sigh of relief at the thought of a bit of peace. She listened drowsily to the sounds of Farmer Tubbs catching up the squealing piglets and putting them into the net-covered back of the pick-up truck, and then the noise of it driving away. She closed her eyes and slept.

A Pig with a Gift

But when she woke later and went outside again, a shock awaited her. Ace had not gone to Market.

"Hullo, Mother," he said.

"Why have you not gone to Market?" asked the sow peevishly.

"I didn't want to. I told you."

"Didn't want to! It's not a question of what you want or don't want, it's what the farmer wants. Why didn't he take you?"

"I told him. He said to me, 'Do you want to go to Market?' and I said 'No'."

"You stupid boy!" said the sow. "How could he have possibly known whether you were saying 'Yes' or 'No'?"

Because I've been training him, thought Ace. Two grunts for a Yes, one grunt for a No. I think he's learned that now.

"And how could you possibly have understood what the man said?" went on his mother. "Pigs can't understand people's talk."

"Can't they?" said Ace.

That's odd, he thought. I can.

"No, they certainly cannot," said the sow. "No pig ever has and no pig ever will. I never heard such rubbish. But I still can't think why he took the rest and left you."

Just then they heard the sound of the truck returning. The engine was switched off, and footsteps approached the sty.

"There!" said the sow with a sigh of relief. "He's come back for you. He must have overlooked you when he was catching them up. You didn't want to go to Market indeed! You stupid boy!"

Farmer Tubbs's face appeared over the pigsty wall.

"Don't look so worried, old girl," he said to the huffing, puffing, grumbly sow. "You'll get your rest all right—I'm taking young Ace away now. Say goodbye to your mother, Ace."

"Goodbye, Mother," said Ace.

"Goodbye," said the sow, and then, feeling she had been a trifle rough on him, added "dear", and "have a nice time", and waddled inside to lie down again.

Farmer Tubbs waited a moment, elbows on the wall top, and looked down at the piglet he had decided *not* to take to market.

"Saved your bacon, I have, for the time being any road," he said. "Not that you could know what I'm talking about. Though I dare say you'll get to know what you're called in a while, like a dog would. Eh? Ace! Ace! That's your name, my lad. The Ace of Clubs. Human beings like playing games, you see, and you can play a lot of different games with a pack of cards. Fifty-two of 'em there are in a pack, Spades, Hearts, Diamonds and Clubs. Though what good 'tis to tell you all that I ain't got no idea."

He opened the door of the sty and came inside, closing it behind him. The last thing he wanted was the piglet loose in the farmyard, dashing about all over the place. He expected that it might be a job to catch it even in the sty, and that when caught, it would squeal and kick and wriggle as its litter-mates all had.

"Steady now," he said as he approached it. "We don't want no fuss."

But Ace stood quite still, allowed himself to be picked up, and made no sound or struggle.

"You'm an extrahordinary pig, you are, young Ace," said Farmer Tubbs as he carried the piglet out.

Because it lay so quietly in his arms (and because it was already quite a weight to carry), the farmer decided to risk putting the piglet down on the ground outside, so that he could bolt the sty door the more easily.

"You sit there a minute, Ace, there's a good boy," he said without really thinking what he was saying, and when he turned round again, it was to find the piglet sitting waiting.

"Well I never! Did you ever?" said Farmer Tubbs. "Anybody would think . . . oh no, don't be so daft,

Ted Tubbs."

He stared at the Ace of Clubs for a long thoughtful minute, and the Ace of Clubs stared back, sitting silently on his hunkers.

Then Farmer Tubbs cleared his throat, nervously

it seemed, took a deep breath, and, turning away, said, "Walk to heel then, Ace," and set off across the yard. Looking down as in a dream, he saw on his left side the piglet marching steadily along, its pink snout level with his heels, the strangely-shaped black emblem upon its flank showing proudly for all to see.

And perhaps because Ace was marching so smartly, Farmer Tubbs was reminded of his own days as a soldier many years before, and he squared his shoulders and threw out his chest and pulled in his stomach. Left right, left right across the yard he went until they came to the door of a loose-box on the far side, and Farmer Tubbs automatically cried "Halt!"

Ace stopped dead.

Inside the loose-box, the farmer sat down hurriedly on a bale of straw. Strange thoughts rushed through his head, and his legs felt wobbly. He licked his lips, and once again taking a deep breath, said in a hoarse voice, "Ace. Lie down."

Ace lay down.

Farmer Tubbs swallowed. He took a large white-spotted red handkerchief from his pocket and mopped his brow.

"Ace," he said. "Listen to me, carefully now. I don't want to make no mistake about this. I don't know if I be imagining things or not. I might be going

around the bend. It might be just a cohincidence, or it might be . . . a miracle. But I got to know for certain sure. So you answer me honestly, young Ace of Clubs, you tell old Ted Tubbs the truth."

He paused, and then very slowly and clearly he said, "Can . . . you . . . understand . . . everything . . . that . . . I . . . say?"

The piglet grunted twice.

CHAPTER 3

A Pig and a Goat

I hope you can understand something that I'm going to say, thought Ace. Pigs are permanently hungry anyway, and he had not had a mouthful to eat since early that morning, long before the farmer had set out for Market. Now he was ravenous, and he let out a short but piercing squeal. Farmer Tubbs had not kept pigs all his working life without learning that a squeal like that meant either fury or fear or hunger. And since the piglet looked neither angry nor afraid, he got the message and hurried out to fetch food.

"He's not as stupid as he looks," said Ace out loud.

"He'd have a job to be," said a voice.

Ace spun round to see, standing in the gloom at the far side of the loose-box, a strange figure. It was covered in long greyish hair that hung down its sides like a curtain, and it wore a grey beard and a pair of sharp-looking curved horns.

The goat walked forward into the light and stood looking down at the piglet.

"What's your name?" she said.

"Ace. Ace of Clubs."

"Funny sort of name," said the goat. "How did you get that?"

Ace turned to show his left side.

"It's because of this mark on me," he said. "It's

something to do with some game that humans play, called cards."

"How do you know that?" said the goat.

"He told me. Ted Tubbs told me."

"Ted Tubbs? Is that his name? How do you know it is?"

Ace felt like saying, "Why must you ask so many questions?" as his mother had, but the goat, with that sixth sense that animals have, continued, "I hope you'll forgive me for asking so many questions, but I'm curious to know how you could possibly understand what the man says."

The look in her golden eyes was kindly and mild.

"I just do," said Ace. "I don't know how. I thought all animals did but my mother said that no pig ever had."

"Nor goat either," said the goat, "nor cow nor sheep nor horse nor hen, to the best of my knowledge. I've lived here all my life, all fifteen years of it, and the only word he says that I can recognise is my name."

"What's that?"

"Nanny."

Just then Farmer Tubbs opened the door and came in carrying a bucket of pigswill. He poured it into a trough in the corner of the loose-box and stood watching approvingly as Ace tucked into it.

"I'll tell you summat, Nanny," he said, patting the old goat's hairy back. "You'm looking at a most extrahordinary pig there. Not just his marking I don't mean—I'll swear blind that pig do understand what I do say to him."

He waited till Ace had licked the trough clean and turned to face him, and then he said, "Now then, young Ace, allow me to introduce you. This is Nanny, and I'm putting you in with her so's she can keep an eye on you and teach you a thing or two. She's brought up ever so many kids, Nanny has, and there ain't much she don't know. She'll be company for you, stop you feeling lonely."

"What was he on about?" said Nanny when the farmer had gone. "I heard my name a couple of times but the rest was just the usual gabble."

"He said you were very wise," said Ace.

"I wasn't born yesterday."

"And he said he was leaving me in here with you. I hope you don't mind?"

"Not a bit," said Nanny. "You'll be company for me, stop me feeling lonely." She pulled a wisp of hay out of the crib and munched it thoughtfully. "How come you never went to market this morning then?" she said. "I looked out and saw a bunch of pigs going off in the truck. Why did he leave you behind?"

"He asked me did I want to go," said Ace, "and I said 'No'."

"You mean to tell me that as well as you being able to understand the man . . . what did you call him?"

"Ted Tubbs."

"As well as you understanding Ted Tubbs, he can understand what *you* say?"

"Only three things," said Ace. "One grunt means 'No', two grunts mean 'Yes', and a sharpish squeal means 'Fetch food'. I think he's learned those all right."

"Going to teach him any more?"

"I don't know really. I suppose I could increase the grunts, three for this and four for that and so on, but I don't know if he could cope with it. What do you think, Nanny?"

"Might be beyond him," said Nanny. "He's not all that bright. Might be better to *show* him what you want."

"Like what?"

"Well, what d'you fancy doing?"

Ace thought.

"I wouldn't mind having a walk round the farm," he said. "You know, have a good look at everything, meet all the other animals. I've been stuck in a sty all my life so far and now I'm shut up in here."

"All right," said Nanny. "So you'd like to get out of this loose-box. I can't open the door, you can't open the door, he can. I can't tell him to open it, you can. By showing him what you want."

"How?"

"Listen," said Nanny, and she outlined a simple plan.

When Farmer Tubbs next opened the half-door of the loose-box and came in to fill Nanny's crib with hay for the night, the old goat bleated. To him it was just a bleat. To Ace she was saying, "Go on. Try it now."

Ace trotted up behind the farmer as he reached up to the crib, and butted him in the back of the leg with his snout.

"What's up with you, Ace?" said Farmer Tubbs, and for answer the piglet went to the door which the farmer had closed behind him, and butted it hard, several times, so that it shook on its hinges.

"You wants me to open it?"

Two grunts.

"Why?"

Ace marched round the box a couple of times, came back to the door and butted it again.

"You wants to go for a walk!" said Farmer Tubbs. "Well I never! Did you ever? What next? D'you want me to come with you?"

One grunt.

"Oh all right, then. But you come back when I calls you, understand?" and reassured by an affirmative answer, the farmer opened the door.

"And he will," he said to Nanny. "You don't understand what I'm saying because you're not all that bright. But that Ace—why, he can do everything bar talk. I suppose you could say he's too clever for words."

CHAPTER 4

A Pig and a Cat

Farmer Tubbs spent a worried time talking anxiously to himself as he went about his chores.

"You'm a fool, Ted Tubbs," he said. "Pigs is for pigsties, not to be let go wandering about wherever they fancies. Don't like to follow him around. Looks like I don't trust him. Whoever heard of trusting a pig, I needs my brains seeing to. But then he might hurt hisself, he might run away, he might get lost. Worth a bit of money a pig that size is, but 'tisn't the value if I'm honest. I've got real fond of that pig."

He kept looking at his watch, forcing himself to allow a full hour to pass, and when it had, he went and stood outside the loose-box, half-hoping that the pig would have made his own way back and be waiting there, safe and sound. But there was no sign of Ace.

Behind him there was a rattle as Nanny put her forefeet up on top of the half-door and peered out.

ACE

"Right then, Nanny," said Farmer Tubbs. "He's had long enough. It'll be dark afore long. We'll fetch him back, shall us?" and he called "Ace!" He waited a minute or two, but the piglet did not appear.

"Coop—coop—coop—coop—coop— come on then!" shouted Farmer Tubbs, the sounds he always made to call cows or sheep or chickens, but though there was some distant mooing and bleating in answer and a few old hens came scuttling hopefully across the yard, Ace still did not come.

"You'm a fool, Ted Tubbs," said the farmer. "What am I thinking of! There's only one proper way to get him back," and he cupped his hands to his mouth and took a deep breath and bellowed the summons that all pigmen have always used over the ages to bring their errant charges hurrying home, curling their tails behind them.

"PIG—pig—pig—pig—PIG!! Pig—pig—pig—pig—PIG!!" roared Farmer Tubbs, and in half a moment there was a distant rattle of little trotters and Ace came in sight, galloping as hard as he could go with that curious rocking-horse action that pigs have.

"What did I tell you!" said Farmer Tubbs triumphantly to Nanny, but inwardly he heaved a sigh of relief as he opened the door and let in the puffing, panting Ace of Clubs.

"Good boy!" he said, patting the piglet (just like he were a dog, he thought). "Good boy, Ace!"

But in reply there was only a rather breathless but none the less urgent squeal, so off he hastened to fetch food.

When the farmer (and the food) had finally disappeared, Nanny said, "How did you get on?"

"I had a lovely time," said Ace. "I made a speech to the sheep, had a conversation with the cows, a discussion with the ducks, a gossip with the geese, and a chat to the chickens. And by the way, you were right, Nanny. I asked all the different sorts of animals if they could understand what Ted Tubbs says to them, and they couldn't. They know some things, like to come when he calls them, but that's about all."

"The cows would know their names, I'm sure," said Nanny.

"Oh yes, they did. Called after flowers mostly, they are—Buttercup, Daisy, Primrose, that sort of thing. But I'll tell you a funny thing, Nanny—all the sheep had the same name."

"Really?"

"Yes. I said to one of them, 'What's your name?' and she said, 'Barbara'. But when I said to the next one, 'And what's your name?' the answer was 'Barbara'. I asked all of them in turn and they all said, 'Baaaabara'."

"How funny," said Nanny, straight-faced.

"Wasn't it?" said Ace.

He yawned hugely and snuggled down in the straw.

"Good-night then, Ace," said the old goat. "Sleep tight, mind the fleas don't bite," but the only reply was a snore.

Full-stomached, and tired out after all his exploring (for his legs were rather short), Ace slept soundly that night. When he woke, it was bright morning and the low early sun was streaming in over the half-door. Ace stood up and shook himself. Under the wooden crib Nanny lay, her jaws going round rhythmically.

"Morning, Nanny," said Ace.

"She can't answer," said a voice.

Looking up, Ace saw that there was a cat sitting on top of the crib. It was a large white cat, with one yellow eye and one green one.

"Why not?" he said.

"Because she's cudding," said the cat. "Chewing the cud. You're not supposed to talk with your mouth full, didn't your mother tell you?"

"No," said Ace. "Why not?" he asked.

"It's rude," said the cat.

At that moment Nanny swallowed noisily and got to her feet.

"Don't tease the lad, Clarence," she said. "He's only young," and to Ace she said, "This is an old friend of mine. His name is Clarence."

"How do you do?" said Ace.

"Pretty well, considering," said the cat.

"Considering what?"

The cat looked narrowly at him.

"MYOB," he said.

"What does that mean?"

"Mind your own business."

"Clarence!" said Nanny.

"Don't mind him," she went on to the piglet. "It's just his manner. He doesn't mean any harm."

"It's NSOMN," said Ace.

"What does that mean?" asked Clarence.

"No skin off my nose."

"But of a clever Dick, aren't you? What do they call you?"

"Ace of Clubs."

The white cat jumped easily down from the crib and walked slowly around the piglet. First he inspected

Ace's right (white) side with his left (yellow) eye, and then the left (marked) side with his right (green) eye.

"I've seen that odd black shape somewhere before," he said.

"It's something to do with a game the farmer plays," said Ace. "With some cards."

"Ah yes, that's it," said Clarence. "He sits down and lays all these bits of card out in rows, I've watched him. He lays them out on the table, some with black marks, some with red, some with pictures."

"Fifty-two of them, there are," said Ace. "Spades, hearts, diamonds and clubs. Funny though, isn't it? I thought you played games with other people—I used to with my brothers and sisters, chasing games, tag, that sort of thing. Strange for him to play on his own. He must have a lot of patience."

"Wait a minute, young know-all," said Clarence. "Are you telling me you've been inside the farm-house?"

"Oh no."

"Then how come you know all this stuff about fifty-two cards and hearts and clubs and all that?"

"He told me. Ted Tubbs told me."

"Ted Tubbs?"

"That's the man's name, Clarence," said Nanny. "You and I have never known what he's called but Ace found out. You see, he understands his language."

"Do you mean to tell me," said Clarence, "that you can understand every word that What's-his-name . . ."

". . . Ted . . ."

". . . Ted says to you?"

"Yes," said Ace. "I thought that all the animals could but it seems I'm a freak."

"You'll have to watch out, Clarence," said Nanny. "Next thing you know, you won't be the only one sitting in a comfy chair in the nice warm farmhouse watching Ted play cards. Ace will be in there too."

Clarence gave a loud miaow of amusement.

"Not for long," he said. "Young know-all wouldn't take much time to blot his copybook."

"What d'you mean?" said Ace.

"Only cats and dogs are allowed indoors, because only they can be house-trained."

"What does that mean?"

With a look of disdain on his face Clarence indicated a large lump of pig dung in the straw.

"You can't go doing that on the carpet," he said. "Or the other."

"Why not?"

"It's rude. Didn't your mother tell you? Humans don't mind if you do it outside but indoors it's simply not done. We cats bury that sort of thing anyway."

"Oh," said Ace. "Does Ted do it outside then?"

"No no no," said Clarence. "He has a special little room with a kind of white chair with a hole in it."

"He's almost as clean as a cat," said Nanny drily.

"That would be difficult," said Clarence smugly, and he leapt neatly on to the top of the half-door and was gone.

Ace thought about all this.

"Nanny," he asked, "are you house-trained?"

Nanny gave a loud bleat of laughter.

"Not likely," she said. "A goat's gotta do what a goat's gotta do!"

"Well d'you think I could be? I wouldn't mind seeing what it's like inside Ted's house. D'you think I could train myself?"

"Ace," said Nanny. "The more I see of you, the more I think you could do most things. Except fly."

CHAPTER 5

A Pig with a Plan

That day, and every day that followed, Farmer Tubbs
let Ace out to run free. At first he bombarded the piglet
with a whole list of Don'ts—don't go too far, don't go
near the road, don't fall in the duckpond, don't chase
the hens and so on. But gradually as time passed and
Ace always behaved himself, the farmer just let him
out without a word, confident now that he would not
get into trouble and would return to the loose-box
when called. It never occurred to him to say, "Don't
go into the house."

In fact, Ace was not in a hurry to do that. He talked
the matter over with Nanny, and she advised against
haste.

"You don't want to rush him," she said. "Having
a pig in the house is not something that humans are
used to. He might take it amiss. And one thing's

40

sure—you've got to keep on the right side of Ted Tubbs."

"What's wrong with being on his left side?" said Ace.

"No, it's just an expression. To keep on the right side of someone means to keep in his good books."

"Good books? I don't understand."

"Sorry," said Nanny. "You're such a bright fellow that I forget how young and inexperienced you are. What I mean is that it's important for Ted to like you, to treat you as a pet."

"What's a pet?" said Ace.

"An animal that people keep for the pleasure of its company, like a dog or a cat."

"Are you a pet?"

"Sort of."

"What about the other animals on the farm—the cattle, the sheep and the poultry?"

"No, they're not pets. They all finish up as meat," said Nanny. "Sooner or later, young and old alike, they're all killed to provide meat for humans to eat."

Ace shuddered.

"My brothers and sisters," he said, "who went to Market . . . ?"

"Someone there will have bought them, to feed them up till they're fat enough to kill. And that could

41

still happen to you, Ace, if you rub Ted Tubbs up the wrong way."

"You mean," said Ace slowly, "if I . . . what was it Clarence said? . . . if I blot my copybook?"

"Exactly," said Nanny. "I'm not saying you won't be able to go into the farmhouse one day if that's what you want to do. But don't try to run before you can walk, don't rush your fences, look before you leap. The first thing to remember is that the farmer is not the only person who lives in that house."

"Why, who else is there?"

"Clarence, and Megan. Now Clarence won't be any problem—I'll have a word with him—but Megan's a different matter."

"Who's Megan?"

"Ted's dog. You may not have seen her. She's not too keen on taking exercise."

"I think I have," said Ace. "Brownish?"

"Yes."

"Short-legged?"

"Yes."

"With big sticking-up ears and a stumpy tail?"

"Yes."

"And very fat?"

"That's Megan. She loves her food, Megan does. She must be the fattest corgi that ever came out

of Wales. Now you'll have to get her on your side.
You see, cats don't really bother about people, they
only care about themselves, but a dog reckons it's
man's best friend. Megan could be very jealous. But if
she takes a liking to you, I think you'll be home and
dry."

"How can I make her like me?" said Ace.

"I'll tell you," said Nanny. "Megan, you see, is the
most tremendous snob."

"What's a snob?"

"Someone who pretends to be much better-bred
than other folk."

"And is she?"

"No, but she looks down her nose at all other dogs.
They are common curs. She (she says), has Royal
blood."

"And has she?"

"Ask her," said the old goat. "I'm not going to tell
you any more about Megan, because the best thing
you can do is to ask her yourself, very respectfully,
mind, and remember to appear tremendously
impressed by what she tells you. Oh, and don't call her
'Megan'. That would be much too familiar."

"What should I call her?" said Ace.

"Ma'am," said Nanny.

*

ACE

With all this in mind, Ace began to make changes in his routine. It had become his habit to make, each day, a grand tour of the farm, chatting to all the other animals (for he was a friendly fellow). Meeting the ducks and geese and chickens was easy for they all ranged freely. As for the cows, the barbed-wire fences that kept them in were no problem to Ace, who ran easily under the lowest strand. Sheep-fencing was a different matter, for by now Ace had really grown too big to be called a piglet and so too fat to squeeze through the wire-mesh. But this was no great loss, since none of them ever said anything to him but "Barbara".

At first he had always visited his mother to say good-morning, but lately he had given this up. For one thing, they could not see each other since the sty walls were too high, and for another she never really sounded pleased about his visits.

"I understood that you had gone to Market," she said when first she heard his voice again. She sounded disappointed. And before long the only answer he received to his cheery greeting was a grunt, so then he didn't bother. Now, he went straight towards the farmhouse as soon as he was let out in the morning, with the idea of meeting Megan in mind.

Behind the house was a piece of lawn bordered by

a shrubbery and in this he hid to watch what went on. It never varied, he found. Each day when Ted Tubbs had finished milking and gone indoors for his breakfast, the corgi would come out of the house on to the lawn and waddle about on the grass, making herself comfortable. If the weather was fine, she would then lie awhile in the sunshine, but any hint of rain or wind sent her hurrying in again as fast as her short legs would carry her stout body.

ACE

For a week or more Ace lay and watched and wondered how best to approach Megan. First impressions, he felt, might be very important. In the event, the matter was decided for him.

He was lying flat in the shrubbery one sunny morning, watching Megan through the leaves, when suddenly a voice said, "Peeping Tom, eh?"

Ace whipped round to see Clarence sitting a few feet away regarding him with a cold green-and-yellow stare.

"I don't know what you mean," he said in a flustered tone.

"Hiding in the bushes," said Clarence. "Spying on a lady. You can't do that."

"Why not?"

"It's rude. Didn't your mother tell you? Just exactly what are you up to, young know-all?"

Ace decided on honesty, not because he was aware that it was the best policy but because he was straightforward by nature.

"Clarence," he said. "Will you do me a favour? Will you introduce me to Megan?"

"Why should I?"

"Well, you see I really am very keen to become a house-pig, you know, live in the farmhouse like you and Megan do. Nanny said that you wouldn't mind but that Megan might not like the idea."

Clarence combed his whiskers thoughtfully.

"You're an odd sort of a chap, you are," he said. "I don't care what you do. As far as I'm concerned it's . . . what was it you said?"

"NSOMN."

"Quite. And you haven't a hope of succeeding, in my view. Never mind what the man thinks of such an idea, I can tell you who won't stand for it, and that's HRH."

"HRH?"

"Her Royal Highness over there—Western Princess of Llanllowell."

"Is that Megan's real name?"

"Oh yes. Registered at the Kennel Club, ten champions in pedigree, all that tosh. It's enough to make a cat laugh," said Clarence, and he stood up and walked out on to the lawn towards the dog, Ace following.

"Megan," he said when he reached her, "this is Ace. Ace—Megan," and he sauntered off, waving his tail.

Ace stood smartly at attention in front of the corgi, his trotters neatly together. Close up, he could see that she was not merely brownish but a fine red-gold colour with a snowy-white chest.

Ears pricked, head raised, she favoured him with an

imperious stare. From her expression you would have thought there was a bad smell under her nose. Ace cleared his throat, and with downcast eyes he said, "Your servant, Ma'am."

CHAPTER 6

A Pig and a Dog

The corgi did not reply.

Glancing up, Ace fancied that the look in her eyes had softened a little. Was that a slight wag of her stumpy tail? Might as well go the whole hog, he thought.

"Please accept my apologies, Ma'am," he said, "for interrupting your walk. May it please Your Majesty."

Now the stump was really wagging.

"There's nice-mannered!" said Megan. "Sick and tired it is we are of being called plain 'Megan' by that cat. Who was it told you that we are of the blood-royal?"

"A friend, Ma'am. Nanny the goat."

"The goat!" said Megan scornfully. "A creature of no breeding whatsoever, look you. Common as muck. Surprised it is we are that she should even be aware of our rank. What did she tell you about us?''

Ace had never heard of the royal 'we', but he was becoming used to the way the dog spoke and to her unfamiliar lilting accent, so different from Ted Tubbs's broad tones.

"She said you had a very good pedigree, Ma'am," he said. "Though I don't quite know what that means, I'm afraid."

"We don't imagine for one moment that you would," said Megan.

She stared pointedly at the mark on Ace's left side.

"You're not pure bred, that's obvious, isn't it?" she said.

"I shouldn't think so," said Ace.

"Don't know anything about your ancestors, we presume?"

"No. Though I'm told my great-grandfather was a sheep-pig."

"Well there you are, see. Doesn't bear thinking about."

"But please," said Ace, "won't you tell me all about your family, Ma'am? If you would be so gracious, Your Majesty."

"There's ignorant you are," said Megan. "There's only one person in the whole country that is properly

addressed as 'Your Majesty', and that is the Queen.
She is the most important human being in the land,
see. Now the point about our family is not merely
to do with pedigree—plenty of dogs have pedigrees
a mile long even if not as distinguished. No, the reason
why we are head and shoulders above all the other
breeds is this. Corgis are the Queen's dogs. Buckingham Palace is bursting with them, and wherever she
goes—Windsor, Sandringham, Balmoral—she takes
them with her. Now the Queen's children are called
'Their Royal Highnesses'. In fact she made her eldest
son the Prince of Wales (because of her fondness for
corgis, no doubt). And so her own dogs are styled
princes and princesses every one, look you. Now it
so happens, see, that we personally are directly related
to the Royal corgis. Western Princess of Llanllowell,
that is our proper title."

"So should I call you 'Your Royal Highness'?" said
Ace.

"No no, that's for humans. Corgis were originally
bred as cattle-dogs, to nip at their heels. Now a tall dog
might get a good kick in the face doing that, but our
breed, see, has nice short legs to keep out of trouble. So
it's plain how you should address me, isn't it now?"

"How?"

"'Your Royal Lowness'," said Megan. "But you

need only do so at the start of a conversation. From then on, 'Ma'am' will suffice."

"Yes, Ma'am," said Ace.

"Now," said Megan, "the audience is at an end. You may attend on us tomorrow."

"Yes, Ma'am," said Ace.

He turned to go, but Megan said sharply, "Backwards, look you."

"Sorry?"

"It is customary to withdraw backwards when leaving the presence of royalty."

Ace could not wait to tell Nanny. He raced back to the loose-box and bashed on the door with his hard little snout so loudly that a puzzled Ted Tubbs came hurrying to let him in.

The farmer leaned on the half-door and looked over at the pig.

"What's the matter, my boy?" he said. "Did summat frighten you?" but receiving only a single grunt in reply, went off again about his business.

"What was he asking?" said Nanny.

"If something frightened me. No no, I was just in a hurry to come in because I've just met Megan and I'm bursting to tell you all about it," said Ace, and he did.

"'Your Royal Lowness' indeed!" said Nanny. "What a fraud! She really gets my goat with all her airs and graces. Are you going to be able to put up with all that stuff, Ace?"

"Oh yes, it's quite amusing really. I didn't realize a snob would be so funny."

"I suppose she said that you were common?"

"Oh yes, and you too."

Nanny gave a snort.

"D'you think," said Ace, "that Megan is really related to the Queen's corgis?"

"Shouldn't think so for a moment. What she has never realized is that it doesn't matter *who* you are. It's *what* you are that counts in this life, and you're worth ten of that silly fat thing. Snobbery apart, she's like all dogs, thinks she can understand what the man says. But like all dogs, she can't. Just a few commands that she's learned to obey, that's about as far as it goes. Now you, you can understand his every word. Did you tell Megan that?"

"No."

There was a scratch of claws on the outside of the half-door and Clarence appeared over the top of it.

"She wouldn't believe you if you did," he said.

"Oh you heard that, did you?" said Nanny.

"Listening in to other people's conversation!" said Ace. "You shouldn't do that, Clarence."

"Why not?"

"It's rude. Didn't your mother tell you?"

Clarence did not answer this. Like all cats, he had the knack of making others feel uncomfortable by simply not reacting, by appearing, that is, to be taking no notice of what has been said. He jumped up on to the crib and began to wash his face, so that now it was Ace who felt that he had been rude by being cheeky. He tried to make amends by making conversation.

"Why wouldn't Megan believe me, Clarence?" he said.

Clarence finished his washing before replying.

Then he said, "Because she only believes what she

wants to believe. Besides, if you succeed in your plan to get into the house, you could have the upper hand of her. You'll be able to understand the man. She won't. It could be amusing."

"Now Clarence," said Nanny. "I know what you're thinking. You'd like to take that dog down a peg or two, wouldn't you?"

Once again Clarence did not answer. He lay down and licked his black nose with his pink tongue. Then he wrapped his white tail around him, shut his yellow eye, shut his green eye, and went to sleep.

Next morning when Farmer Tubbs came out of the house after breakfast, he saw a strange sight. Sitting close together in the middle of the lawn were his dog, his cat and the Ace of Clubs. Anyone would think, he said to himself, that all three of them were household pets.

"You'll have to watch out, Megan, and you, Clarence," he said. "Next thing you know, you won't be the only ones sitting in comfy chairs in the nice warm farmhouse, watching me play cards. Ace will be in there too," and he walked away chuckling to himself at so ridiculous an idea.

CHAPTER 7

A Pig in the House

The farmer's words, Ace could see, were received quite differently by the other two animals. Clarence took absolutely no notice but stared absently into the distance. Megan looked up at the man, her ears flattened, and wagged her whole rump in pleasure at the sound of his voice.

Pity she can't understand what he said, thought Ace. She might ask me in. Ted's left the door wide open too. How am I going to wangle an invitation? He caught Clarence's eye (the yellow one, as it happened) and once again that telepathic sense that humans seldom, but animals so often, possess, came into play.

"He's left the door open," said Clarence. "Care to have a look round the house, Ace?"

"Oh could I?" said Ace. Clarence had never before called him by name, and he warmed to the white cat.

"You most certainly could not!" barked Megan

sharply. "A pig in the house! There's ridiculous! We never heard of such a thing!"

"I just thought you might like to show Ace your trophies, Megan," said Clarence smoothly.

The corgi's expression softened.

"Trophies?" said Ace. "What are they?"

"Awards that Megan won at dog shows," said Clarence. "Prize-cards, rosettes, that sort of thing."

"And a cup," said Megan. "You're forgetting that we won a cup in our younger days."

"So you did," said Clarence. "A little silver cup. Well, silvery-coloured anyway. Ace would be ever so interested, wouldn't you, Ace?"

"Oh yes, yes, I would! You must be very proud, Ma'am, to have won these things."

"We hardly expected to lose," said Megan, and she got up and waddled off into the farmhouse.

"Come on," said Clarence. "That's tickled her vanity. I knew it would. Follow me now, and don't speak till you're spoken to."

Inside, he led the way down a passage and into the living-room. On either side of the fireplace were two armchairs, and in the smaller one Western Princess of Llanllowell already lay in regal state.

On the wall beside this chair were fastened three cards, coloured red, with black writing on them, and

pinned to each card was a blue rosette. On the mantel-
shelf above the fireplace stood, amongst other knick-
knacks, a very small cup, of a size suitable to contain
a sparrow's egg.

Megan glanced up at these objects.

"The Royal Collection," she said offhandedly.
"Beautiful, isn't it now?"

"Oh yes, Ma'am," said Ace in reverent tones. "It is
an honour to see them." See them he could, but read
what was written on them he could not. The inscrip-
tion on the three prize-cards was in fact identical except
for the dates, which spanned three successive years.

VILLAGE FETE
NOVELTY DOG SHOW
CLASS 10—FATTEST DOG
FIRST PRIZE

On the little cup was engraved:

DOG DERBY
ANY VARIETY 200 YARDS RACE
BOOBY PRIZE

"Impressive, aren't they?" said Clarence. He winked
(the green eye) at Ace.

"Oh yes!" breathed Ace.

"Gracious of Her Lowness to compete, don't you think?" said Clarence, shutting his yellow eye.

"Royalty has its obligations, look you," said Megan modestly. "*Noblesse oblige.*"

She settled herself more comfortably in the armchair.

"The cat will take you on a conducted tour," she said. "We hope your feet are clean."

"Oh it was a scream. Nanny!" said Ace that evening, back in the loose-box. "Clarence just went out of the room of course, but I could see Megan watching me out of the corner of her eye so I walked out backwards. 'What does *noblesse oblige* mean, Clarence?' I said when I caught him up.

"'It's foreign talk,' he said.

"'What sort?' I said.

"'Double Dutch,' he said.

"So I wasn't any the wiser."

"Never mind," said Nanny. "What happened next?"

"Clarence showed me all over the house."

"Upstairs too?"

"Yes, though that was difficult. The stairs are steep. Megan can't get up them at all, Clarence says, she's too stout. I saw the bedrooms, and a room with a big white trough in it."

"That would be the bathroom," said Nanny.

"Yes, that's it, that's where Ted washes himself, and there was one of those white chairs with a hole in the middle of it too. There was another one in a very small room downstairs."

"You didn't . . . do anything, I hope?" said Nanny.

"Do anything?"

"Yes, you know . . ."

"Oh no," said Ace. "I went out on the lawn. 'I'll be in the kitchen when you've finished', Clarence said to me. He's nice when you get to know him, Clarence, isn't he?"

"Yes," said Nanny. "He lives in the kitchen, I know. He has a bed right by the Aga cooker, he's often told me how cosy it is in there on winter nights."

"That's right," said Ace. "I saw some other downstairs rooms but the kitchen's lovely, full of nice food smells. But still I think the living-room's the place for me, even though it means putting up with Her Lowness."

"Why?"

"Because in the living-room Ted Tubbs has got the most amazing thing, Nanny. You just can't imagine what an extrahordinary thing it is."

"What is?"

"The magic box!"

"Magic box?" said Nanny. "What are you talking about, Ace?"

"Well," said Ace, "when we'd finished the tour of the house we went back into the living-room and Megan asked Clarence if he'd showed me everything and Clarence said, 'Yes,' and Megan said, 'Upstairs too?' And then Clarence stared at her in that way he has and said, 'Oh yes, Your Lowness, the stairs weren't too high for Ace,' and Megan said, 'We are not amused,' and Clarence said, 'A cat may look at a princess,' and climbed into the other armchair.

"I waited a bit but neither of them said any more. In fact they both went to sleep, so I thought maybe I'd outstayed my welcome. But just as I was going out of the room I saw this thing in the corner. A big box it was, only one side was nearly all glass, like a window. So I walked up to it and had a look in this window but all I could see was myself looking back."

"That would be your reflection," said Nanny. "Like you get if you look in a puddle or in the duck-pond. Nothing magic about that."

"No, but wait," said Ace. "Below this glass window there were some knobs sticking out. So out of curiosity I pushed one of these knobs with my snout, and you wouldn't believe what I saw then, Nanny!"

"What did you see?"

"Inside that box," said Ace slowly and impressively, "there was a man, talking! He was talking about all kinds of different things, and as well as the man there were loads of different pictures, and the man talked about them too. Megan and Clarence didn't take a bit of notice, I suppose because they wouldn't have understood what the man was saying. But I could, of course, and it was ever so interesting, Nanny, honestly! I tell you, I simply couldn't take my eyes off that magic box!"

Thus it was that Farmer Tubbs, his morning's work finished, came in to his living-room to find the Ace of Clubs sitting on his hunkers in front of the television set, watching the BBC *One O'Clock News*.

CHAPTER 8

A Pig and the Television

After that, life was never really the same again for Farmer Ted Tubbs. All that afternoon he talked to himself in a bemused fashion.

"That pig," he said, "he were sat there watching the telly! Must have switched it on himself. Never seed such a extrahordinary thing. I couldn't think of nothing to say. In the end I says to him, 'Anything interesting on the news then, Ace?' and he gives a couple of grunts, so I didn't like to turn it off. I goes and has my bit of lunch and when I comes back he's sat there watching *Neighbours*. What next, Ted Tubbs, what next?"

So stunned was the farmer by the pig's actions that the idea of forbidding him the house in future never crossed his mind, especially as, in the days that followed, Ace behaved faultlessly. All he did was to watch a great deal of television. He damaged nothing and made no messes anywhere (for Farmer Tubbs had the sense always to leave the garden door open: he himself often did not bother to take off his wellies when he came in, so a few muddy trotter-marks did not signify). And at tea-time, before the farmer came in after finishing the afternoon milking, the pig would switch the television off with a prod of his snout, leave the house, and make his way back to the door of the loose-box. Here, if Farmer Tubbs did not hurry, a loud squeal would tell him that Ace wanted to be let in, fed, and left to spend the night with his friend Nanny the goat.

"Just as well, I suppose," the farmer said to himself (and to Megan and Clarence, though his reasoning meant nothing to them), "because if he stopped in the house we'd have the telly on all night long. 'Tisn't that I don't enjoy some programmes, but when there's rubbish on I likes to switch off and have a nice game of patience. Now if that pig was in nights, he'd be watching the *Midnight Movie* and then he'd have ITV on till 'twas time for milking again."

In point of fact, Ace was becoming very selective in his viewing. He had not been a house-pig many days before he found out, first by chance and then by trial and error, that pressing each of the five knobs below the window of the magic box produced a different result. One turned the thing off, and the other four controlled BBC 1, BBC 2, ITV and Channel Four. Ace of course had no idea that there were such things as different channels, but he soon found that the magic box offered a choice of pictures. His sense of time was good too, and before many weeks had passed, his viewing had taken on a definite pattern.

By experimenting with the control knobs, Ace found what programmes suited him and at what time of day. These, generally, were split into two parts, morning viewing and afternoon viewing. In between, he took a nice long nap, lying on the hearth-rug. He had the sense not to attempt to get into either of the armchairs.

For his morning watching, that is between the hours of roughly nine o'clock and eleven o'clock, he usually chose BBC 2. At this time there was a programme for schools called *Daytime on Two*, where there were items on such things as Science, Mathematics and a section called *Look and Read*. All of these Ace found fascinating, though on occasion he would switch to Channel Four's *Our World*, where there was often interesting information about Food.

In the afternoon, say between four o'clock and half-past five, he enjoyed Children's TV on either BBC or ITV. There were always plenty of animals, either live or in cartoons, and their antics amused him.

But though the afternoon's viewing was for fun, the morning's, because of his unique gift for understanding the human tongue, was, for Ace, highly educational, especially with regard to number and to language. Quick to learn, he began to recognise simple words. There were, for instance, items about Road Safety, using diagrams with large lettering, and soon Ace, had he been called upon, could have distinguished a sign that said STOP from one that said GO.

Soon too, he acquired a basic grasp of figures, becoming aware, for example, that he had one snout, one tail, two eyes, two ears and four legs, and that the sum of himself and the other two animals was three.

At first he feared that they might object to his generous use of the television set. By good fortune, however, he found that, though in general they were not interested, certain items appeared which were popular with them.

Clarence enjoyed the cat food advertisements in the commercial breaks on ITV, particularly one which showed a large white cat very like himself that fished meat from a tin with one paw, in the most elegant manner.

As to Megan, luck had it that quite early on, BBC 1 showed a repeat of a programme about the day-to-day life of the Royal Family. There were pictures of the Queen and her husband and her children and her grandchildren, at Buckingham Palace, at Windsor, at Sandringham and at Balmoral, and everywhere she was surrounded by corgis.

The moment Ace heard the programme announced, he woke Megan.

"Quickly, Your Lowness, quickly!" he cried. "The Queen is in the magic box!" and there, sure enough, she was, in the opening shot, walking in her garden with no less than six corgis.

Megan's growl at being disturbed changed to an eager whine.

"Oh there's lovely, see!" she said excitedly. "Our Aunt Olwen, that is, by the Queen's feet, we're nearly sure! And the one behind her looks ever so like our Cousin Myfanwy!"

She watched spellbound as the TV programme continued, silent except for an occasional yap at recognising an uncle or a grandparent, and when it was all over she actually, for the first time, addressed the pig by his name.

"Our thanks to you, Ace," she said graciously. "We shall be obliged if in the future you will draw our attention to any more pictures."

"Of the Royal Family, you mean, Ma'am?" said Ace.

"Of our royal family, yes. If the Queen appears without them, don't bother to wake us."

None of Ace's viewing bothered Ted Tubbs, for he was always busy about the farm. Like all farmers, he could not treat Sunday as a day of rest. The cows still needed milking morning and evening, babies were born regardless of the day of the week, and all the animals needed bedding, food and water. But Farmer Tubbs did treat Sunday differently in one way. He always tried to finish his morning's work by about eleven o'clock, and then he set about preparing and cooking himself a large traditional Sunday lunch.

It never varied. Roast beef and Yorkshire pudding, roast potatoes and green vegetables and lashings of thick gravy, followed by a jam roly-poly. And while this was cooking, the farmer would pour himself a quart mug of cider, and, sitting in the larger of the two armchairs with his feet up, would drink it slowly with much lip-smacking and a belch or two for good measure.

But on the very first Sunday after he had discovered Ace watching telly, the scene in his living-room was different.

Anyone looking in through the window would not have been surprised to observe the farmer in one chair and his dog in the other, but might well have been amazed to see, sitting at the farmer's side, a sizeable young pig, a white pig that bore on its left side a curious mark shaped like the Ace of Clubs.

Farmer Tubbs took a pull at his cider and addressed his house-pig.

"Now then, Ace," he said, "I bin telling myself, these last few days, that maybe old Ted Tubbs is going around the twist. You was sat in front of the telly when I come in t'other day, there's no doubt of that. And the telly was switched on, there's no doubt of that. But I must have left it running. I can't believe as 'twas you as switched it on."

He took another drink, nerving himself for what he had to do.

"I got to find out for sure," he said. "I don't never have the thing on this time of a Sunday, so I don't know what rubbish they be showing, but lunch won't be ready for another half-hour, so we might as well turn it on. Or rather you might as well turn it on, Ace. I hopes you can, for my peace of mind."

He raised his mug, took a long swallow, and then, pointing at the television set, said in as firm a voice as he could manage, "Switch it on, Ace. Any channel will do."

Later on, when Ace's morning lessons had taught him to read, beneath the control knobs, the numbers 1, 2, 3, 4 and finally the word OFF, he might have selected a channel. As it was, with luck once again on his side, he simply walked over to the set and pushed the middle one, 3.

"The time," said the announcer in the ITV studios as he swam into sight, "is exactly twelve-thirty. Time for our regular Sunday programme especially for those of you who earn their living from the land. Sit back and put your feet up and, for the next half-hour, enjoy *West Country Farming*, followed by the *Farmers' Weather Forecast*."

Ted Tubbs's mouth fell open. He stared in wonderment at Ace.

"Well I never!" he said. "Did you ever?"

CHAPTER 9

A Pig in a Pick-up

On a Sunday evening some months later, Ace lay in the straw of the loose-box, telling Nanny, as he always did, about the day's viewing.

No longer did he refer to 'the magic box'. He had learned that what he was watching was a television set, which could show pictures of things that were happening all over the world and indeed from space. How the television did this remained to him, as it does to most humans, a mystery, but he did not worry his head about that. It was full enough already of ideas and impressions and new-found knowledge.

Much of what he told the old goat meant little or nothing to her. Her experience of life was, after all, very limited, for she had never moved a step outside Ted Tubbs's farm; but she listened with interest to his stories of strange lands and peoples and customs and a host of other things shown on the schools programmes.

ACE

This particular day being a Sunday, Ace and Ted had, of course, watched *West Country Farming* while the lunch was cooking, and now the pig could not wait to tell Nanny all about the programme. It had upset him deeply. Indeed he left half his supper untouched, and his voice trembled as he told of what he had seen.

"Oh it was horrible, Nanny!" he said. "The first part wasn't too bad, it was about a market. I used to think that my brothers and sisters had gone to a town called Market, but these were pictures of pigs, sheep and cattle in pens, and people offering money for them. 'Bidding', it's called—the one who offers the most money gets the animals. I must say I'm glad I didn't go to market, but at least all the beasts there were still alive and well. But the second half of the programme—ugh!"

It wouldn't be true to say that a shudder ran through Ace's body. His flesh was much too solid for that, but if he could have shuddered, he would have.

"Why?" said Nanny. "What was it about?"

"An abattoir!" said Ace in a funereal voice. "A slaughterhouse, where animals are taken to be killed. They didn't show that bit, thank goodness, but they showed all the bodies. Rows and rows of them there were, all hanging head down, strung up by their back legs, cattle, sheep and pigs."

"Goats?" said Nanny.

"Don't think so. The cattle and the sheep weren't too dreadful because by then they were just sides of beef or carcasses of lamb, but the pigs still looked like pigs; dozens of them there were hanging there, all scrubbed and cold and still. I shan't sleep a wink tonight."

"Humans have always killed animals," said Nanny.

"Not only animals," said Ace gloomily. "You should just watch the television. Humans spend a lot of time killing other humans."

"Not for food, surely?" said Nanny.

"No, I don't think so, but the news is nearly always about people getting killed. Sometimes they do it on purpose, with guns and bombs, and sometimes they get killed by mistake on trains or aeroplanes or on the roads. And as well as that there are natural disasters, like earthquakes and floods, when thousands of people die."

"Sounds very depressing, watching television," said Nanny.

"Oh it isn't all like that," said Ace. "Sometimes it's quite funny. There's a cartoon programme that Clarence specially likes, called *Tom and Jerry*."

"Who are they?"

"Tom's a cat and Jerry's a mouse."

"Another programme about sudden death?"

"No, because you see Tom is stupid and Jerry's very smart, so Jerry always gets the best of things. Clarence likes the bits where Tom gets his tail caught in a door or gets beaten up by a bulldog, that sort of thing."

"Don't you ever feel," said Nanny, "that you'd like to stay in and watch the evening programmes? Or stay the night perhaps? I mean, don't think I'm trying to get rid of you—I love having you here—but there must be a lot of television you've never seen yet."

"No thank you," said Ace. "I did stay a bit later than usual one evening—it was after *Tom and Jerry* and Clarence was telling me at length how he would deal with Jerry and what a dumb cat Tom was—and I found that it's about then that Megan wakes up. She sleeps most of the day, but when it's getting near her supper-time she comes to life, and oh Nanny, she's such a *bore*! On and on about all the Champions in her pedigree and how her nephew won at Cruft's and

her niece was presented at Court and what the Queen Mother is supposed to have said to her Uncle Gareth. No wonder Clarence goes out every evening. No, daytime viewing is enough for me, and anyway I like talking it over with you afterwards. But I hope I don't have nightmares tonight. Ugh! That abattoir!"

"Look, Ace," said Nanny. "I am a great deal older than you. Which doesn't make me wiser, because you've already learned a whole host of things about the world that I had no idea of. But I do know one thing, which is this. Worrying does no one any good. Hundreds of thousands of pigs may get slaughtered, but you won't. With a bit of luck you and I are both going to die quietly and peacefully in our beds of old age. I shall die before you, just because I am a great deal older, but I don't worry about it. So finish your supper."

"I think I will," said Ace, and he did.

"Now then," said Nanny, "come and lie down."

She settled herself near him, but not too close, for he had grown so heavy.

"I shan't sleep," said Ace.

"Try counting sheep," said Nanny. "Live ones. That'll send you off."

"I don't think it will," said Ace, but it did.

Though Ace did not exactly have any nightmares, he did have a strange dream. He dreamed that he was riding in Farmer Tubbs's pick-up truck. The farmer was driving, and he, Ace, sat next to him on the passenger's side, held there by some kind of arrangement of straps. Where they were going he did not know, but in the dream he was able to get his tongue round some of the words of the English language that he had come to recognize on the *Look and Read* programme.

"Where are we going, Ted?" he said, and the farmer replied, "To market."

Two days later, a Tuesday, it was market day, and Ace stood in the yard, watching idly as Farmer Tubbs came out of a shed carrying a calf, which he put under the net in the back of the pick-up. Then he looked at Ace. Then he said, "I be going to market, Ace. Want to come?"

Remembering his dream, Ace replied with a single explosive grunt, a very definite "No!"

But by now, after many months of communication with the pig, Farmer Tubbs was completely confident that Ace understood every single word he said, in a way that no dog, let alone Megan, ever could, not even the most intelligent dog in the world. Now he came up to Ace and fondled the roots of his big ears, something that he knew the pig greatly enjoyed.

"Now you listen here, my boy," he said. "There ain't no need for you to come if you don't want to. I just said to myself, 'Ted Tubbs', I said, 'maybe Ace would enjoy the ride. And 'twould be company'. Now I reckon I know what's worrying you. You think I might be going to sell you, isn't that it?"

Two grunts.

"Never, Ace, never," said Farmer Tubbs earnestly. "You got my solemn oath on it. I won't never part with you and that's a promise. You believe that, don't you?"

Two grunts.

"That's all right then. Now then, time I was off," said the farmer, and he opened the passenger door.

"You coming?" he said, and to his delight Ace, with a final couple of grunts, jumped into the truck and sat upright while Farmer Tubbs carefully fastened the seat-belt around his fat stomach.

CHAPTER 10

A Pig in a Pub

The first pair of eyes to see Ace as he rode along in state in the pick-up truck were very short-sighted ones. They belonged to an elderly lady who was the village gossip. She lived with her sister in a cottage beside the road that led from the farm to the market town. All day she sat, and peered out between her lace curtains, minding everyone else's business.

"Quick!" she called as the pick-up approached. "Look at this!" but by the time her sister arrived, the truck had passed.

"Oh you're too late!"

"What was it?"

"Ted Tubbs on his way to market, I recognized his truck. And what d'you think, he had a woman with him! He's kept that quiet, hasn't he? These old bachelors! You can't trust them!"

"What did she look like?"

"Well I couldn't see her face too well, my sight's not what it was, but I can tell you she was a big stout piece, and no beauty neither."

A small boy playing in his front garden on the left-hand side of the road was the next to see Ace. The pig's bulk hid the man from the child's sight, and, greatly excited, he ran indoors, crying, "Mummy, Mummy, I've just seen a pig driving a lorry!"

"Don't be silly," said his mother.

"I did! I did!" yelled the boy angrily.

"Don't tell lies," said the mother, "and don't you shout at me like that," and she thumped him.

ACE

A minor accident was the only further thing that happened on the journey to market. A motorist approaching traffic lights suddenly caught sight of Farmer Tubbs's passenger. Goggle-eyed, he turned his head to watch them pass, and ran neatly into the back of the car ahead.

When Farmer Tubbs arrived in town and reached the market, he drove the pick-up into the car-park. This was close to the tavern, a pub called The Bull, used by all the farmers, dealers and drovers to quench their thirsts on market days.

"Now," said Farmer Tubbs to Ace, "I has to take this here calf in, and then I shall have a look around and see what the trade's like. So will you be all right stopping here for a bit?" And when he received the usual affirmative answer, he undid Ace's safety straps for greater comfort, and then, shutting the door, made off with the calf.

Ace looked all about him with curiosity, but though he could hear a good deal of mooing, bleating and grunting, he could not see much of interest through the windscreen except lots of cars, trucks and Land Rovers.

Presently, for something to do, he moved along the bench-seat and arranged himself on the driver's side. Often, on a Saturday, he had watched Formula One motor-racing on BBC's *Grandstand*, and though the pick-up was hardly a Grand Prix car there were certain likenesses. It had a steering-wheel, and a gear-lever, and an instrument panel. Raising his front legs, Ace rested his trotters on the steering-wheel, and gave himself up to a daydream of being the world's first Formula One pig racing-driver.

At that moment a red-faced man came rather unsteadily out of The Bull and began to weave his way across the car-park.

"Why, if 'tisn't old Ted Tubbs!" he cried as he neared the pick-up, but then the colour drained from his cheeks, leaving them as grey as cold porridge, and he staggered away, murmuring to himself, "Never again! Not another drop!"

After an hour or so, Farmer Tubbs returned. Though he had left the windows of the truck a little open, he found Ace panting, for the metal cab was not the coolest of places on a warm day.

"You'm hot, Ace!" said the farmer. "You'm thirsty too, I dare say?" and Ace assured him, in the normal way, that this was indeed the case.

"Tell you what," said Farmer Tubbs. "I always has a drink in The Bull afore I goes home on market day. You come in along of me, and we'll ask the landlord for some water for you. I gotta bucket in the back."

Thus it was that the patrons of the public bar at The Bull were treated to the sight of Farmer Tubbs entering with a large pig at heel.

"Now now, Ted," said the landlord. "You can't bring him in here. You seen the notice on the door."

"I did, Bob," said Ted Tubbs. "'No Dogs allowed', it says. This here's a pig."

"That's true," said the landlord thoughtfully. "The usual for you then? Half of scrumpy?"

"If you please," said the farmer.

Farmer Tubbs was a very moderate drinker. Cider was his tipple, but only on Sundays before lunch did he allow himself that quart mug. A half-pint was his usual ration, especially on market days when he was driving.

"What about your friend?" said the landlord.

The farmer held out his bucket.

"Put some water in here, will you, Bob?" he said.

"Go on, Ted!" someone shouted. "Buy 'im a beer. You can't bring the poor beast into a pub and not give him a proper drink."

"He shall have one on the house," said the landlord, and he drew a pint of beer and poured it into the bucket.

Ace, who had been listening carefully to these exchanges, noted with pleasure that the name on the

pump handle was that of a brand highly recommended
in the television advertisements.

He bent his head to the bucket.

The beer looked good.

He put his snout in the bucket.

The beer smelt good.

He drained the bucket.

The beer tasted good.

He gave a short happy squeal, and it was obvious to everyone what he meant.

There came a chorus of voices.

"He liked that!"

"That were a drop of good stuff, old chap, weren't it?"

"Same again, that's what he's saying!"

"He could do with the other half!"

"And one for the road!"

And the drinkers in the public bar rose, to a man, and poured their tankards of beer into Ace's bucket.

Almost before Farmer Tubbs had tasted his half-pint of scrumpy, the pig's bucket was empty again, and when they left, it was with some difficulty that the Ace of Clubs managed to get back into the pick-up truck.

"Good job you're not driving," said the farmer as he strapped the pig in.

Ace hiccuped.

At first the drive home was uneventful, but then Fate decreed that a police car should come up behind them just as Farmer Tubbs swerved wildly across the road. He swerved because Ace had fallen asleep and, despite the seat-belt, had lurched against him.

Next moment there came the sound of a siren, and then the police car, lights flashing, pulled in front of the pick-up and forced it to a stop.

One of the two policemen in the car got out and walked to the driver's side of the truck. Farmer Tubbs wound down his window. The smell of beer in the cab was overwhelming.

"Good-afternoon, Sir," said the policeman in the coldly polite way that policemen have on these occasions. "Having trouble with the steering, are we?"

"'Twasn't my fault," said Farmer Tubbs. "'Twas the pig."

"I see," said the policeman. He produced his breathalyser kit.

"Now, Sir," he said, "I'm going to ask you to blow into this tube. If you look at this machine, you'll see that there are three little lights on it—just like traffic lights, green, amber and red. Now then, Sir, if the green light comes on when you blow, that means you have had no alcoholic drink at all."

"Well I have had," said Farmer Tubbs. "A half of scrumpy, in The Bull."

The policeman raised his eyebrows at this. He wrinkled his nose at the reek of beer drifting out of the window.

"In that case," he said, "the amber light will come on. This is to show that you have drunk alcohol in some shape or form. But if, after forty seconds, that amber light should go off and the *red* light come on, then, Sir, you will be over the limit and I shall have to ask you to accompany me to the station for a blood test."

Farmer Tubbs shook his head in pity.

"You'm barking up the wrong tree, young man," he said. "I shan't never be over the limit."

"Just blow, Sir," said the policeman. "We'll see."

So he did, and they did.

The amber light came on. The policeman watched, waiting for it to give way to red, confident that here was yet one more drunken driver. A half of scrumpy indeed! But after forty seconds the amber light went out and no red light appeared.

"Told you," said the farmer.

"I don't understand it," said the policeman. He went and fetched the second constable from the police car.

"The stink of beer in here's enough to knock you down," he said to his mate.

"'Tis the pig," said Farmer Tubbs.

At this point Ace awoke, roused by the sound of voices. He looked happily at the six men he could see, four policemen and two Farmer Tubbs. He gave an enormous belch, and both policemen reeled backwards.

"Well I never! Did you ever?" said Farmer Tubbs. "Ace, you've been and gone and made a proper pig of yourself!"

CHAPTER 11

A Pig in an Armchair

"Tell you one thing," said Farmer Tubbs as they drove on home. "With all that beer inside you, I reckons you better go straight in the loose-box. We don't want no accidents in the house, do we, Ace?"

Ace let out two sleepy grunts. He had meant to give a single one but he seemed not to be quite in control of things.

"Oh no we don't!" said Farmer Tubbs, and when they reached the farm he drew up outside the loose-box door.

"It don't matter," he said, "if you wets your bed in here."

Nanny was peering out.

"He's had a skinful, Nanny," said the farmer. "One over the eight."

Once the safety-belt was undone, getting out of the truck was more a matter of falling out for Ace, and

90

he walked into the loose-box in a rather wobbly way. Nanny bleated anxiously.

"Don't you worry," said Farmer Tubbs. "He'll be all right when he's had a good sleep."

Ace did indeed fall fast asleep.

While he slept, Clarence came visiting.

"Oh Clarence, I'm worried!" said Nanny. "There's something the matter with Ace. He isn't acting at all naturally. What can it be?"

Clarence was a cat of the world. More than once he had courted the Blue Persian at the local pub, and the smell of drink was familiar to him.

"He's had a skinful, Nanny," he said. "One over the eight," and when the simple old goat still looked mystified, Clarence explained.

"Today," he said, "this little piggy went to market, and by the look of things, he's drunk a good deal of beer. He'll be all right when he's had a good sleep."

Neither farmer nor cat was quite correct. Ace did have a good sleep, but when he woke he was not quite all right. He had a hangover.

"Oh Nanny!" he groaned. "I've got an awful headache!" and after a while he explained all that had happened.

"I must have drunk a whole bucketful," he said.

"Why did you drink so much?" asked Nanny.

"I was so thirsty. And it did taste nice. But now I wish I hadn't."

"Well, you've learned a lesson," said Nanny. "A little of what you fancy does you good. But you can have too much of a good thing."

Clarence was in the kitchen when Ace went into the farmhouse the following morning. He got out of his bed by the Aga and walked round the pig, looking critically at him with first the green and then the yellow eye.

"Better?" he said.

"Oh yes thanks, Clarence," said Ace. "I'm afraid I made rather an ass of myself."

"Difficult for a pig," said the white cat. He sat down in front of Ace and gave him a quizzical green-and-yellow stare.

"Seen Megan yet this morning?" he said.

"No. Why?"

"She was wondering where you'd got to yesterday."

"Did you tell her?"

"Stupidly, I did."

"Why 'stupidly'?"

"Because I suspect Her Lowness is just longing to take you to task about your behaviour," said Clarence.

He gave a fair imitation of Megan.

"'Going into a public house, look you, and drinking too much, see! There's *common*!' I should stay out here and give her a miss if I was you."

"Oh but it's Wednesday," said Ace.

"So?"

"There's *Paddington Bear* on BBC 1. I always watch that."

"I wish you luck," said Clarence.

Ace tiptoed into the living-room, hoping to find Megan asleep. She was, so he switched on BBC 1 very softly; he had long ago learned to turn the volume control with his teeth. But before Paddington could appear the telephone rang, something that always woke the dog, for she considered it her duty to boost its tones with a volley of barks.

This double summons brought Farmer Tubbs in from the yard, and when he had gone out again after answering the call and leaving mucky wellie-marks all across the carpet, Megan lost no time in speaking.

"We want a word with you, boyo," she said sharply.

The old Ace would have replied to this in the meek respectful way in which he had long been used to speaking to the corgi. "Yes, Your Lowness?" he would have said, and perhaps added, "What is it, Ma'am?"

But now a sudden flame of rebellion burned in Ace's broad breast. You stupid pompous little beast, he thought, with all your airs and graces, speaking to me as if I were no better than a . . . than a dog. Western Princess of Llanllowell my trotter! Why, you're just a mouthy little Welsh cow-hound. What am I doing kowtowing to you? And he did not answer.

"Did you hear what we said?" snapped Megan.

"Not now, Megan," said Ace firmly. "I'm busy."

There was a short stunned silence before the Western Princess found her voice.

Then, "Upon our word!" she spluttered. "'Not now' indeed! 'Busy' indeed! 'Megan' indeed! You will kindly address us in the proper fashion."

At that moment Paddington appeared on the screen in his funny blue hat.

"Oh shut up!" said Ace, and turned the volume up full.

"Oh Nanny, you should have seen it!" said Clarence that night. Often he came in the small hours for a chat with Nanny, who, like many old folk, did not sleep too well. Now he had jumped up to his usual perch on the crib, whence on occasion he launched himself upon an unwary loose-box mouse. Ace was fast asleep in the straw.

"Megan was jumping about in her chair," Clarence went on, "yapping her head off, practically frothing at the mouth, and Ace just turned his back on her and

sat watching till his programme was over. Then he switched it off and turned round.

"'What was it', he said very quietly, 'that you wanted to say to me?'

"Well by now her ladyship was so hopping mad at being treated so disrespectfully I thought she was going to have a fit.

"'How dare you tell us to shut up!' she yelled. 'How dare you!'"

"And what did Ace say to that?" said Nanny.

"Oh it was great!" said Clarence. "He got up and he walked slowly over to where she was sitting, in the smaller of the two armchairs, and he said, still very quietly, 'I'll tell you how I dare. It is because I have suddenly realised that I am no longer a little piglet, bowing and scraping to you, and having to listen to you waffling on about your piffling pedigree and your rotten relations and what the Princess of Wales said to your Great Aunt Fanny. I am now a large pig, about ten times as large as you, and I am fed up to the back teeth, of which I have a great many,' (and he opened his mouth wide) 'with all your silly snobbish nonsense.'"

"And what did Megan say?" asked Nanny.

"He didn't give her a chance to say anything," said Clarence. "He did all the talking. 'Now', he said,

'I want to watch *Time for a Story* on Channel Four, and I do not wish to be interrupted. On second thoughts, get out of this room. Just push off, quick!' and he gnashed his teeth together with a very nasty noise that sounded like 'Chop-chop! Chop-chop!' I shouldn't think Megan's moved so fast for years. She couldn't exactly put her tail between her legs, there isn't enough of it, but she was out of that room like a . . . like a . . ."

". . . scalded cat?" said Nanny.

"Exactly. And," said Clarence, "—and this is the best bit—Ace switched on Channel Four, and then he climbed up into Ted's big armchair and sat there watching. Then after the programme was over and all was quiet again, Megan came slinking back. Oh Nanny, how are the mighty fallen! She stuck her head round the door and gave a little whine, as if to say 'Please, can I come in?'"

"What did Ace say?" asked the old goat.

The white cat looked down with a certain fondness at the sleeping pig, the strange black mark on his side rising and falling to the rhythm of his breathing. Clarence was not one to give his affection easily, but he had grown to like the Ace of Clubs.

"I thought he handled it beautifully," he said. "He could have gone on being tough with her—'I'm bigger than you, watch your step', that sort of stuff. Or he could have got a bit of his own back on her for the way she's always patronized him—teased her or sneered at her for her high-and-mighty ways. But no, he just said, quite firmly but in a kindly voice, 'Come in, Megan. I've something to say to you.'

"'Yes, Ace', said Megan, rather uneasily. You could see she was expecting him to tell her off again, but instead he said, 'There's a documentary about Cruft's Dog Show on the telly this afternoon, they've just shown a clip of it and there were quite a lot of corgis there. I wondered if you'd like me to switch it on for you when the time comes?'"

"What did she say?" asked Nanny.

"She looked at him," said Clarence, "just like she looks at her master. She put her ears flat and she wagged her rump and she said in a humble voice, 'Oh we should like that, Ace! There's kind of you.'

"Oh I wish you could have seen him, Nanny, sitting in that big armchair, looking for all the world like Ted Tubbs's twin brother. He sat there staring down at Megan, and what d'you think he said, to round it all off?"

"What?"

"'There's a good dog, Megan. There's a good dog.'"

CHAPTER 12

A Pig in the Papers

On market day the following week, the public bar at The Bull was, as usual, full of farmers and dealers and drovers. In addition there was a very young man who had just started in his first job as a cub reporter for the local newspaper, the *Dummerset Chronicle*.

One of his duties was to cover the market and take note of the fatstock prices, not the most interesting of work. So that he pricked up his ears, as he sat in a corner nursing a glass of shandy, at a conversation between the landlord and some of the customers.

"Ted Tubbs been in with that pig, Bob?" asked one.

"Ain't seen him today," said the landlord.

"I never seen nothing like that afore," said another.

"A pig, drinking beer like that!" said a third.

"I reckon he put down more than eight pints," said the landlord.

"He had a skinful," said the first man. "One over the eight."

A pig drinking beer, said the reporter to himself. Though he had not been long in the job, he knew that an interesting item of news which you got before anyone else was called a 'scoop', and he hastily swallowed his drink and hurried off to the newspaper offices.

"It might make a story," said his editor in the tired bored way that editors have. "Go and see this Farmer Tubbs and find out what you can."

When the cub reporter arrived at the farm and rang the front doorbell, no one answered. This was partly because Farmer Tubbs was busy with the afternoon milking, and partly because the bell hadn't worked for years. So the reporter walked round the side of the farmhouse, where he found the garden door open. Someone had the television on, he could hear, so he walked in, calling, "Hallo? Excuse me! Can I come in?"

From the nearest room a dog barked, but then came the sound of a single loud grunt and the dog immediately fell silent.

Nervously, for he felt that perhaps he had already gone too far, the young man opened the door of the room.

Though in later years, as a much-travelled newspaper man, he saw many strange sights in many strange countries, he never forgot the scene that now met his eyes.

On the television was the cartoon *Tom and Jerry*.

Directly in front of the set sat a white cat, its tail swishing angrily (for Jerry had just caught the tip of Tom's tail in a mousetrap).

In a small armchair lay a very fat corgi.

In a big armchair sat a large pig.

All three were watching the cartoon.

All three took not the slightest notice of him.

"Oh I like *Tom and Jerry*!" said the cub reporter. "Can I watch, please?" and almost as though it was some sort of reply, the pig grunted twice.

"Who was that?" said Ace, when the young man had left to try to find the farmer.

"Haven't a clue," said Clarence, and, "We don't know, we're sure," said Megan.

"He likes *Tom and Jerry* anyway," said Ace.

"How do you know?" said Megan.

"He said so."

"Of course!" said Megan. "We were forgetting," for she now knew of Ace's great gift. The old Megan would never have believed in the possibility of such a thing. The new, Ace-worshipping Megan had no doubt at all of his powers.

Across the yard, the hum of the milking-machine suddenly stopped.

"I'm going for my supper," said Ace. "Shall I switch the telly off?"

"Sure," said Clarence, and, "There's kind of you!" said Megan, so he did.

Hardly had the reporter found the farmer and introduced himself than there came the sound of a loud urgent squeal.

"Just a minute, my lad," said Farmer Tubbs. "Time and tide and Ace wait for no man," and he hurried off to fetch the pig's supper.

The old man and the young leaned on the half-door of the loose-box, watching.

"He's enjoying that," said the cub reporter. "Is there any beer in it?"

"Bless you, no!" said Farmer Tubbs. "Why ever . . . ? Oh I see. You've heard tell, have you? When he had a few, in The Bull?"

"Yes. And I'd like to do a story on it, for *The Chronicle*, if you don't mind, Mr Tubbs. A pig that drinks beer, that'll make a nice little item, half a column maybe, and it'd be quite a scoop for me. I've not been long in the job, you see."

"Who told you?" asked the farmer. "The police?"

"The police? No, I heard it in The Bull. What's the pig's name, by the way?"

"The Ace of Clubs."

The reporter looked at the mark on the pig's side.

"Oh yes, I can see why," he said. "If I write about it, it would be good publicity for you, Mr Tubbs. You should get a really good price for him then."

"I shall never sell him," said Farmer Tubbs. "He's a pet. A house-pig, that's what he is."

"That reminds me," said the reporter. "You must have left your TV set running. I couldn't get an answer so I went in through a side door and the pig was watching TV, along with your dog and your cat."

"He enjoys a bit of telly," said the farmer.

"That'll make the story even better. You'll be telling me next that he selects the channels and switches it on himself, ha, ha!"

"Ha, ha!" said Farmer Tubbs.

"By the way," said the reporter, "the pig was sitting in an armchair, your armchair, I dare say."

"Ah, now that explains something," said the farmer. "Lately I said to myself, 'Ted Tubbs, you must be putting on weight something cruel—the springs in this chair have gone flat. You'll have to go on a diet,' I said. Ah well, that's a relief."

By now Ace had finished his supper. He stood and

looked up at the two men with bright eyes that had in them a look of great intelligence, and when Farmer Tubbs said, "Did you enjoy that, old chap?" he grunted twice.

"Anyone would think he could understand what you were saying!" said the reporter.

If only you knew, thought the farmer, but you ain't going to. You can write a piece about him having a drink or watching the telly, but nobody except me is ever going to know that my Ace do know every word that I do say to him. Folk would never believe it, any road. They'd take me away from here and put me in the funny farm.

"You write your piece, young man," he said, "and mind and let us have a copy."

And sure enough the very next day a copy of the *Dummerset Chronicle* was delivered to the farm.

At lunchtime that day Ted Tubbs read this out to Ace (who later translated it for Clarence and Megan, and that evening, for Nanny).

"I shall have to have that framed," said the farmer, "and put on the wall alongside Megan's prize-cards. Pity they never done a photograph. I'd like to have a good one of you."

The very next day Farmer Tubbs's wish was granted, for a phone call came from one of the national

A pig in a million

Of all the pigs in England's green and pleasant land, surely none can compare with the Ace of Clubs, belonging to local farmer Ted Tubbs.

Not only does Ace have the freedom of Mr Tubbs's picturesque old farmhouse, he also enjoys watching television, sitting at his ease in the farmer's armchair.

The Ace of Clubs has been to market, but only as a passenger in Farmer Tubbs's truck. Not only does his unusual pet enjoy the outing, he also savours a refreshing drink of ale at the market's popular hostelry, the Bull Inn. But not for Ace the pint pot. He drinks his beer by the bucket.

"I'll never part with him," Farmer Tubbs told our reporter. "He's a pig in a million."

daily newspapers, wanting to send an interviewer and a photographer; and in due course a large section of the British public opened their copies of the *Daily Reflector* at breakfast time to see a fine picture of Ace, carefully positioned in profile to show his distinguishing mark to best advantage. The picture was accompanied by a generous, if somewhat inaccurate, piece which stated that Ace drank a gallon of beer with every meal, that he not only sat in an armchair but slept in the spare bed, and that his favourite programmes were *University Challenge* and *Mastermind*.

But this was not all.

A week later the BBC rang.

"Mr Ted Tubbs?" said a voice.

"Speaking," said the farmer.

"This is the producer of *That's The Way It Goes*."

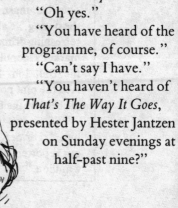

"Oh yes."

"You have heard of the programme, of course."

"Can't say I have."

"You haven't heard of *That's The Way It Goes*, presented by Hester Jantzen on Sunday evenings at half-past nine?"

"Oh bless you, young man, I don't watch telly that time of night. I be abed by nine. I has to get up early to milk the cows. Early to bed, early to rise, makes a man healthy and wise if it don't make him wealthy."

"Well this won't exactly make you wealthy, Mr Tubbs," said the producer, "but we can offer you a fee and certainly pay all your expenses for first-class travel and four-star accommodation if you and your pig would be willing to come to London."

"Whatever for?"

"Why, to appear on *That's The Way It Goes*. Hester Jantzen is greatly looking forward to interviewing you both."

"Well I never!" said Farmer Tubbs. "Did you ever?"

CHAPTER 13

A Pig on the Stage

A little later there came a letter from the BBC, giving date and times and various arrangements. Farmer Tubbs told Ace all about it, and afterwards Ace told his friends.

"What d'you think!" he said excitedly to Clarence and Megan. "Ted and I are going to London!"

"To see the Queen, is it?" cried Megan.

"No, no, we're going to be on the telly. Just think, you'll be able to sit here and see us on the box."

"Except that we can't switch the thing on," said Clarence.

"I'll show you how to do it, Clarence," said Ace. "Look, just put your paw on this knob—where it says 'One'—and push. See?"

"How in the world are you going to get to London, Ace?" asked Megan. "It's a long way, look you."

"Oh the BBC is fixing everything," said Ace.

"They're sending one of the big estate cars that their film crews use—Volvos they are, you've seen them on the telly ads, there'll be loads of room for me in the back—and that will take us straight to the studios. Then when we've done the programme, they've booked a room for Ted for the night, in ever such a posh place."

"Buckingham Palace?" said Megan.

"No, no, a big hotel, near Regent's Park."

"Where will you sleep?" asked Clarence.

"Well," said Ace, "they seemed to think I might not be happy in the hotel, so I shall be sleeping in the London Zoo. Remember, you've seen pictures of it on the telly? And in the Zoo they have what they call Pets' Corner. That's where I'm going. And then next morning we'll be picked up and driven back home again."

"That's all very well," said Megan with a return of some of her old spirit, "but who'll be looking after us?" (And by 'us', she meant, of course, herself.)

"One of Ted's friends is coming in," said Ace, "to do the milking on Sunday afternoon and Monday morning, and feed all the animals. It'll be a lovely break for Ted."

Because for many months now the dog and the cat had had so much explained to them of what appeared on television, they were able to imagine what Ace would be doing. But trying to explain things to Nanny was not so easy.

"They're going to put me on the television," he said to her that evening after supper.

Nanny of course had never in her long life set hoof inside the farmhouse, so that the only idea of the television she had was what Ace had originally told her—it was a big box with one side nearly all glass, like a window.

"Put you on the television?" she said. "But surely you'll smash the thing? It'll never bear your weight."

Ace tried his best to explain to the old goat all that was going to happen, but so many words that he used—'Volvo', 'London', 'studio', 'cameras', 'hotel', 'Zoo'—meant nothing to her.

"Oh well, just as long as you enjoy yourself, Ace dear," she said, "that's all that matters."

And enjoy himself the Ace of Clubs most certainly did when the day came.

What a day it was!

First, there was the journey. His trips in Ted Tubbs's rattlebang old pick-up truck had not prepared Ace for the luxury of travel in a huge, modern, warm, silent, comfortable car speeding eastwards along the motorway; and because of his modest ability in reading and number and his interest in Road Safety programmes on the box, there were many signs and notices that caught his eye; though one, at roadworks, puzzled him. DEAD S OW, it said, and the missing L led him to fear the worst.

Oh but when they reached London—the streets, the houses, all the thousands of buildings! Their numbers filled him with amazement. In all his six months of life he had only been in two houses, a private one—the farmhouse, and a public one—The Bull, and he stared in wonder at the acres of concrete and tarmac.

But London, he could see, was not completely built over. There were a number of large grassy spaces with fine trees, and as they passed through one of these Parks, Farmer Tubbs asked the driver to stop for a moment. It occurred to him that this Hester Jantzen

person might not be best pleased if Ace should have an accident during the interview, and so he let him out for a little walk.

Then at last they arrived at the BBC Studios!

How the onlookers gaped as the pair of them stepped from the staff car to make their entry.

Ted Tubbs was dressed up to the nines. Bathed, and shaved so closely that his chins bore several little cuts, he had attired himself in his best. Not only was his shirt clean but it had attached to it something he never normally wore—a collar. More, he had put on his one and only tie (a black one, so useful for funerals), and in place of wellies he was shod in a pair of old but well-polished black leather boots.

But the crowning glory was his suit. It was his only suit, of a colour best described as sky-blue, that he had bought as a young man. There was no hope of buttoning the jacket, though by letting the back-straps of the waistcoat right out, he had been able to do that up. As to the trousers, most of the fly-buttons were safely in position, and, where the top ones refused to meet he wore, concealed beneath the waistcoat, a carefully attached short length of binder-twine.

And if the man was at his smartest, what of the pig?

Ace positively shone. Not only had Farmer Tubbs hosed him down and soaped and scrubbed him all over, but then, when the soap was rinsed away and Ace had dried in the sunshine, the farmer had produced a big bottle of vegetable oil and oiled the pig all over.

Gleamingly clean, the single mark on his left side showing up more blackly than ever under its sheen, Ace marched proudly into Reception at his master's heels, and they were conducted to the Hospitality Room.

Farmer Tubbs was asked what he would like to drink.

"You won't be on camera for a while yet," they said. "So can we offer you some refreshment?"

It being Sunday, Ted had had his quart of cider before lunch as usual, but he felt thirsty after the journey, and anyway it struck him that a drink might lend him Dutch courage, for he was nervous.

"Well thank you," he said. "I'll have a half of scrumpy."

"Sorry?" they said.

"Cider," he said. "Dummerset cider. We come up from Dummerset where the cider apples grow. And the pig'll have a pint of best bitter."

The cider, when they brought it, was horrid, weak, sweet stuff, but Ace had no complaints about the beer. They poured it into a bowl for him and he thoroughly enjoyed it. But he remembered Nanny's words—

"A little of what you fancy does you good. But you can have too much of a good thing"—and when they offered him another pint, he just gave one grunt.

"He don't want no more," said Farmer Tubbs. "And neither do I."

For a while longer they waited in the Hospitality Room (whence all but they had fled). Farmer Tubbs grew steadily more nervous. The sweet cider had done him no good. Ace on the other hand was on top of the world. The pint of beer had made him feel happy and carefree, and he could not wait to go in front of the cameras. The thought that many millions of people would be watching did not worry him, because he didn't realize they would be. He was simply thinking of Clarence and Megan at home, hoping that Clarence would remember to switch on, and only sorry that dear old Nanny wouldn't see him.

So that when they came to the Hospitality Room to tell Ted Tubbs it was time to go on stage, Ace hurried out ahead of his master. Brushing past the guide who was to take them to the set of *That's The Way It Goes*, he heard a woman's voice saying, "And now, ladies and gentlemen, allow me to introduce . . . [that's me, he thought, and pushing through some curtains, arrived on stage just as a lady with her back to him completed her introduction] . . . Farmer Ted Tubbs!"

ACE

There was a huge roar of laughter from the studio audience as a large pig appeared.

Hester Jantzen (for it was she) clapped her hand to her mouth in astonished embarrassment, and a second roar of laughter came as Farmer Tubbs, helped on his reluctant way by a push, arrived on the stage looking, apart from his clothes, like the pig's twin brother.

Hester Jantzen took her hand from her mouth and smiled, revealing, Ace could see, a fine set of teeth. She was dressed in a silk frock of a shade of emerald green that clashed horribly with the farmer's sky-blue suit, and for a moment it seemed as though a clash of a different kind might occur; for Farmer Tubbs did not know why everyone was laughing at him, and whatever the reason, he did not like it. Already nervous, and uncomfortable in his too-tight clothes, he now felt the heat of the studio lights, and his red face turned redder still.

Miss Jantzen, professional to her painted finger-tips, took command of the situation. Gliding forward, she shook the farmer's large sweaty hand, and said with another flashing smile, "Welcome to *That's The Way It Goes*, Mr Tubbs. How good of you to come, and to bring your famous pig, the Ace of Clubs."

She turned to camera.

"Many of you watching," she said, "will have read

in the newspapers about Farmer Tubbs's pet, Ace to his friends. We've had some unusual animals on *That's The Way It Goes* before, but never one as big, I think."

She made a half move as though to give Ace a pat as he stood patiently in the middle of the stage, but the sheen of oil on his bristly back deterred her, not to mention his size. His teeth, she noticed, were even larger than her own.

"He's a whopper, Mr Tubbs," she said with a light laugh. "How heavy is he?"

"Ten score," grunted the farmer.

"Ten score? What does that mean?"

Farmer Tubbs took out a large spotted handkerchief and mopped his streaming brow. These London folk, he thought angrily, they don't know nothing.

"Don't you know what a score is, young woman?" he said.

"Why yes, twenty."

"Well now we're getting somewhere," said Farmer Tubbs. "A score be twenty pound, so ten score be two hundred. Not difficult, is it, really?"

The audience roared.

Now they were laughing at her, not him, and he sensed this. He began to think he might enjoy himself, and Miss Jantzen sensed that.

"Silly me!" she said. "Tell us some more about him.

I'm told he likes a drink of beer. Would he like one now?"

"He's had one, out the back," said Farmer Tubbs. "That's enough to be going on with."

Hester Jantzen put on her most roguish smile.

"Just as well," she said. "We don't want this little piggy to go wee-wee-wee all the way home."

"Don't you fret, young woman," said Ted Tubbs. "He'm house-trained, like you and me."

When she could speak above the studio audience's laughter, Hester Jantzen said, "I'm told that the Ace of Clubs does a number of remarkable things, apart from beer-drinking, such as sitting in an armchair watching television?"

"He's a extraordinary animal," said the farmer.

"I can see that. People don't realize how knowing pigs are. I believe it was Sir Winston Churchill who said, 'A dog looks up to man, a cat looks down to man, but a pig will look you in the eye and see his equal'."

"He knowed a thing or two, old Winnie did," said Farmer Tubbs. "You have a good look in Ace's eyes, young woman. You'll see what he meant."

Gamely, Miss Jantzen forced herself to approach the Ace of Clubs. They stared at one another, and it was she who looked away first.

"He has a look of great intelligence," she said a little shakily. "Tell us, Mr Tubbs, what else can Ace do?"

"Whatever I wants him to."

"You mean, like sitting down or lying down or coming when he's called?"

"Them's easy things," said the farmer. "Sit down, Ace," and Ace sat down.

"Take the weight off your feet, my lad," and Ace lay down, on his left side as it happened.

There was loud applause from the studio audience, and Hester Jantzen clapped her hands.

"Roll over, Ace," said Farmer Tubbs, "and show them how you got your name," and as Ace obeyed, one of the cameramen quickly zoomed in to show a close-up picture of that extremely unusual single black marking for all the millions of viewers to see.

"Good boy," said Farmer Tubbs. "Now in a minute or two, I want you to go over to Miss Wozzername there and say, 'Thank you for having me'."

"You're not going to tell me," giggled the presenter, "that Ace can speak!"

"No, nor fly neither," said the farmer, "but he'll shake hands with you. Go on, Ace, say 'thank you' to the lady."

And then, before the wondering gaze of the studio audience and of all the viewers across the length and breadth of the country who were watching *That's The Way It Goes*, the Ace of Clubs walked solemnly across the stage, and sitting down on his hunkers, raised one forefoot and politely offered his trotter to Hester Jantzen.

Bravely, the lady grasped it.

"Goodbye, Ace," she said. "I do hope you've enjoyed yourself. Have you?" and the pig grunted twice.

CHAPTER 14

A Very Important Pig

As soon as the BBC staff car dropped them back at the farm on the Monday morning, Ted Tubbs hurried to change into his greasy old overalls and his dungy old wellies, to go round and make sure that his animals had not suffered any harm while in the charge of a stranger.

Ace made his way to the living-room, where he found Megan alone.

"Hullo, Megan!" he cried. "We're back! Did you enjoy the programme?"

"Indeed to goodness, no!" said Megan.

"Why not?"

"Never saw it, see. Clarence must have pressed the wrong knob. Sat there for ages waiting for you to appear, we did, and all they showed was a lot of cowboys and Indians."

Later, when the cat appeared, he favoured the pig with a rather cold green-and-yellow stare, as though daring him to mention the matter, so Ace didn't. But Fortune decreed that nothing was lost. When Farmer Tubbs came in for his lunch, he switched on the BBC *One O'clock News*, and farmer, pig, dog and cat sat and watched as, at the end of it, the newsreader said, "Finally, for those who say the News is all doom and gloom nowadays, here is a clip from last night's edition of *That's The Way It Goes*," and there was Ace having his trotter shaken by Hester Jantzen.

"A nationally-known celebrity," said the newsreader, "greets a brand-new one."

In the days and weeks that followed it became apparent just what a celebrity Ace had become. Only once, many years before, had a pig appeared on TV and attracted anything like as much publicity, and that was when Ace's great-grandfather had defeated all the best dogs in the land to win the Grand Challenge Sheepdog Trials.

Farmer Tubbs was bombarded with letters and phone calls. Fan letters made up much of the mail, addressed to:

> The Ace of Clubs
> c/o Mr T. Tubbs

and as well as invitations to Ace to open fêtes or even new supermarkets, or to appear at functions as a VIP

(Very Important Pig), there were many offers to buy him for large sums of money, from farmers everywhere and from more than one circus proprietor. There was also an offer of marriage (for Mr T. Tubbs) from a lady in Weston-super-Mare.

But Farmer Tubbs refused all these things.

The thought of parting with his pig never crossed his mind.

"You got your health and strength, Ted Tubbs," he told himself, as he finished the afternoon milking one day, "and you got your livestock to see to, and your pets—old Nanny and Megan and Clarence and above all that there Ace of Clubs. What good would any amount of money be to you if you had to part with him? Why, you wouldn't have no one to watch *West Country Farming* with. You wouldn't have no one to keep you company in the old pick-up. You wouldn't have no one to enjoy a drink with at The Bull."

He switched off the milking-machine, and almost at once he heard, from the direction of the loose-box, a short but piercing squeal, a squeal that he well knew was not of fury or of fear but of hunger, and he hurried away obediently to prepare a bucket of pigswill.

As for Ace, success did not spoil him. He had his friends, his favourite television programmes both educational and entertaining, his occasional pint, his comfortable bed. After supper that evening he lay thankfully down in it, ready for a good twelve hours of sleep. It was odd, but he always slept on his right side, as though to show to all whom it might concern that mark emblazoned on his left.

"'Night, Nanny," he said, yawning.

Dimly he heard the old goat reply, as she always did, "Sleep tight. Mind the fleas don't bite," and then, with a last couple of grunts, the Ace of Clubs drifted happily into dreamland.

Noah's Brother

Dick King-Smith

Illustrated by
Ian Newsham

Chapter One

'Brother!' shouted Noah in his great booming voice.

'Yessah?'

'I'm going to build a boat. A big one. 300 cubits long, 50 wide, 30 high. Three decks. Out of gopher wood.'

'That will need an awful lot of trees, Noah. Who's going to cut them all down?'

'You are,' said Noah.

It is an interesting fact (which few people know) that Noah had an older brother. Quite a bit older, actually, since Noah was 600 years old and his brother 708.

Everybody knows who eventually sailed in the Ark: there was Noah and Mrs Noah, their three sons Shem, Ham and Japheth, and Mrs Shem, Mrs Ham and Mrs Japheth; and, of course, two of every animal on earth. But down below, in the lowest, darkest part of the belly of the Ark, was someone else: Noah's brother.

Hazardikladoram was Noah's brother's real name, but nobody in the family ever called him that; it was much too much of a mouthful and besides, everyone had a particular way of addressing him. Noah always called him 'Brother', Mrs Noah only ever said 'Hey, you', and as for Shem, Ham and Japheth, they had invented a nickname for their uncle while they were still quite small.

They soon noticed that whenever their father (who was a huge, bearded, bossy old man) spoke to his brother (who was a small, bald, timid old man), it was to give him some kind of order.

'Do this! Do that!' said Noah to his brother, and always Hazardikladoram meekly answered, 'Yessah!' So the boys took to calling him 'Uncle Yessah', and later, when they were grown up and married, just plain 'Yessah'.

Yessah felt pretty fed up, the morning that Noah told him to start cutting down gopher trees. It

wasn't the work he minded – he was pretty fit for his age – it was the way the family treated him. He grumbled to himself in between swings of his axe:

'I shouldn't mind a "Please" (thunk), or a "Thank you" (thunk) and a bit of respect (thunk). After all, I am the oldest (thunk) member of the family,' and on the word 'family' he gave the gopher tree a specially hard wallop and it fell down.

As it fell, two white doves fluttered out of its branches.

'Oh sorry!' gasped Yessah, who was very fond of animals and had a special way with them, 'didn't know you were up there, my dears.'

The doves flew down and perched, one on each of Yessah's thin shoulders.

'Peace,' said one softly in his left ear; 'Goodwill,' said the other in his right; and then they flew gently away, wing-tip to wing-tip, cooing sweet nothings to one another.

Yessah suddenly felt much happier, and began

chopping down gopher trees right, left and centre.
How I do like animals, he thought as he worked;
and it was just as well he did, for in a few weeks
Noah gave him another order.

By that time the Ark was pretty well finished. To
be fair, the rest of the family had worked hard too:
while the women busily prepared great stores of
food, Noah and his three sons collected all the
trees that Yessah had felled, and sawed them into
planks. They had a lot of fun building the boat,
though there was one job they did not fancy, which
was covering every bit of the boat with pitch to

make it watertight. The pitch was horribly black, thick and sticky, so they gave the job to Yessah.

Then one morning, when everything was ship-shape at last, Noah stood on the poop-deck of the Ark and shouted, 'Brother!'

'Yessah?' said Yessah, hurrying aft.

'Listen carefully, Brother,' said Noah. 'I want two of every kind of animal on the earth. Every beast, every bird, every creeping thing. Two of each. One male, one female. Get it?'

'Yessah. But who's going to collect all that lot?'

'You are,' said Noah.

Chapter Two

'But why do you want them all?'

'That,' said Noah, 'is my business, Brother. You just round 'em up.'

Yessah went off, shaking his head. 'First he builds a whopping great boat miles from the sea, and then he wants to collect two of every kind of animal. Whatever for?'

Yessah hurried back to Noah.

'You're not going to eat these animals, Noah, are you?' he said.

It is an interesting fact (which few people know) that Noah's brother was a vegetarian. All the rest of the family gorged themselves daily on the meat of ox and sheep and goat, but Yessah had never harmed any animal, much less killed one in order to swallow its flesh.

Now, though the crown of his head was only as

high as the tip of Noah's beard, he faced up to his younger brother bravely.

'Because if you are, you can count me out.'

'Brother,' said Noah in quite a quiet voice, 'I give you my word that not one of the animals going into the Ark will be killed. Anyway, Mrs Noah's got a galley full of fresh meat.'

Yessah shuddered, but Noah did not notice because he was staring at the sky. For months it had been blue and clear, but now suddenly, as Yessah saw when he followed his brother's gaze, there were one or two clouds about; they were rather sulky-looking little black clouds.

'D'you think the weather's going to break?' he said.

Noah looked down at him and frowned. His voice suddenly grew much louder.

'I don't think,' he said, 'I know! And if you don't get a move on, and start collecting those animals, something else is going to break – your neck! GET ON WITH IT!'

'Yessah!' said Noah's brother.

*

At first he found the job fairly easy. He began by catching animals that couldn't argue about being caught; and soon there were pairs of creatures like worms and snails and beetles and frogs wriggling, crawling, scurrying and hopping up the gangway into the Ark.

Shem, Ham and Japheth took turns to stand on guard and make sure these early arrivals did not turn round and wriggle, crawl, scurry or hop straight off again.

But when Yessah began tackling some of the larger animals, he met with opposition. Not surprisingly, none of them wanted to volunteer.

Stubborn ones like donkeys refused to listen to him, bad-tempered ones like camels told him to get lost, and intelligent ones like the great apes wanted to know why.

'Give us a good reason, Yessah,' said a big silver-backed gorilla, 'for agreeing to be shut up in a stuffy old boat. We're perfectly happy as we are. Why do you need us?'

'I don't know,' said Yessah uncomfortably, 'only Noah knows.'

'Oh, Noah!' said the gorilla in a rather scornful voice, and he walked away, chewing a bamboo shoot.

'What am I going to do?' said Yessah to the two white doves, Peace and Goodwill, who now went everywhere with him, perched on his thin shoulders. 'How can I persuade the animals to come into the Ark if I don't know why Noah wants them? There must be a reason but he won't tell me.'

'Leave it to us, Master,' said Peace.

'We'll ask around, Master,' said Goodwill.

'We'll ask all the other birds,' they said.

They began by asking the owl, believing him to be wise.

'Why d'you think Noah's doing this?' they said.

'Who,' said the owl.

'Noah.'

'Who who,' said the owl.

Peace and Goodwill looked at each other and shook their heads.

They asked the guinea-fowl, but he only said, 'Go back! Go back!' They asked the bunting, but he only said, 'A little bit of bread and no cheese!' And they asked the song-thrush, but he only said, 'Did he do it? Did he do it? Come out! Come out!'

They asked the kittiwake who said, 'Kittiwake!' and the peewit who said, 'Peewit!' When they asked the kookaburra, he burst into fits of laughter, and

the ostrich said nothing because his head was buried in the sand.

At last, very tired, Peace and Goodwill came across a yellow-billed cuckoo.

It is an interesting fact (which few people know) that the yellow-billed cuckoo's other name is the rain-bird, because when he's noisy it means there's going to be a downpour; and this one was making a tremendous racket.

The doves listened carefully to what he was saying, and then flew back to Yessah, who was gingerly shoving a couple of hedgehogs up the gangway.

'Master! Master!' they cried. 'We've found the reason! We know what the Ark is for. It's going to rain and rain and rain, for forty days and forty nights, and the whole earth will be flooded!'

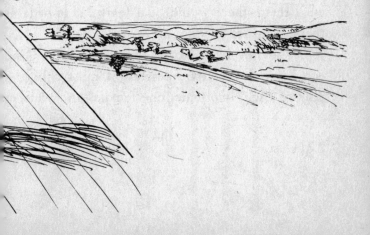

'Who told you?'

'The rain-bird, Master,' said the white doves.

Yessah had been so busy trying to round up animals, he hadn't had time to think about the weather. Now he looked up at the sky and saw that it was filled with clouds, huge angry clouds. At the same moment a huge angry face appeared high above him on the Ark.

'Get on with it, Brother!' yelled Noah. 'We haven't got a quarter of the animals yet!'

Wearily, Yessah set off again. His heart was heavy. If the rain-bird was right, and he did not doubt this, all the beautiful animals on the earth would be drowned, except for two of each sort. He understood Noah's plan now. But how was he to choose which pair, of hippos or kangaroos or antelope? Once they all knew of the terrible danger that threatened them, there would be a fearful stampede as they all rushed for the safety of the Ark.

'It's awful,' he said, 'but only two of each kind can be told, secretly. Somehow I must choose a pair of each, one male, one female, and whisper the news of the coming Flood in their ears.' He looked again at the darkening sky. 'But how can I possibly do this in time?'

'You can't,' said Peace.

'But we can,' said Goodwill.

'How?'

'Simple,' they said. 'We'll ask help from all the birds who don't care tuppence about a flood – the ducks and the geese and the swans, the seagulls and the cormorants and the albatrosses. None of them need to come into the Ark.'

'We'll divide the job up amongst them,' said Peace, 'so that one pair of every kind of animal is told.'

'Except the fish,' Goodwill added, and off they flew.

Before long Noah and his family began to see pairs of animals on the move everywhere. Two by two they came: down from the mountains or out of the forests or across the plains, and they all went into the Ark. Up the gangway they went; lions and tigers, wolves and bears, elephants and giraffes,

one male and one female of every kind. Yessah
stood at the foot of the gangway, ticking off their
names on a long list that he had made.

Last but one a pair of tortoises lumbered slowly
up, just ahead of a couple of hares who had stopped
for a nap on the way.

Out of the gathering gloom two white shapes
dropped down and settled on their master's thin
shoulders.

Yessah shouted up to his brother standing on the poop-deck high above.

'That's it, Noah,' he called, 'that's the lot,' and even as he spoke a big drop of water plopped down on his bald head, and then another. Suddenly the storm broke and the rain came down in torrents.

Above the noise of the wind and the downpour came the sound of Noah's great voice.

'Pull up the gangway!' he shouted, and Shem, Ham and Japheth pulled it up.

'Hey!' cried Noah's brother as the storm roared. 'Hey! Hang on a minute! What about me?'

But nobody seemed to hear.

Chapter Three

Within a few moments Yessah looked like a drowned rat; within an hour he would certainly have looked like a drowned man, so quickly did the Flood rise, if Peace and Goodwill had not flown into the Ark for help. Even so, it was a very close thing.

Once the gangway had been raised there was no way for Yessah to get aboard. Even the port-holes of the lowest deck were far above his head. The water rose to his waist, to his chest, to his chin, until at last he stood on tiptoe, his head thrown back. As he gulped what he felt to be his final breath, he saw the doves peering out.

'Rescue's on the way, Master!' they called. 'Start swimming!'

'I can't swim!' they heard him cry, and then the swirling waters closed over his bald crown.

They say when people are drowning, the whole of their past lives flash through their minds. Yessah's whirling thoughts had got as far as the birth of his baby brother, Noah (when he himself had been a youngster of 108), and then suddenly something very thick and very strong curled itself around his body, and plucked him from the depths.

When Yessah came to, he was lying flat on the planking of the Ark's lowest deck. A ring of assorted faces peered down at him, including two worried little white ones.

'Master!' cried Peace and Goodwill. 'Are you all right?'

'What . . . how . . . who . . .?' spluttered Yessah.

'It was one of the pythons,' said Peace. 'It swam out and coiled itself round you, and hoisted you aboard.'

'And then,' said Goodwill, 'one of the elephants sucked most of the water out of you with its trunk, and one of the gorillas thumped your chest to get your heart beating again.'

Yessah struggled into a sitting position. He

felt sore inside and out but very glad to be alive.

'Oh, thank you all,' he said, 'especially the python. Where are you, my dear?'

'Here,' said a voice, and a great flat blunt-snouted face pushed itself forward.

'You saved my life!' exclaimed Yessah.

'Makes a change,' said the python. 'One of my ancestors spoiled the life of one of yours.'

'Who was he?'

'Chap called Adam,' said the serpent.

At that instant they all felt the deck move beneath them. The Ark was afloat.

High above on the poop-deck, Noah and his three sons felt the movement and peered overside through the rain-filled darkness. They had loaded the Ark carefully, putting all the heavy beasts like elephants, hippos and rhinos on to the lowest deck, and the boat seemed to be riding steadily.

'Get hold of your uncle,' said Noah, 'and tell him to go below to make sure everything's water-tight.' He strode off.

Shem, Ham and Japheth looked at each other.

'Oh Lord!' said Shem.

'Clean forgot about the old geezer,' said Ham.

'He'll be food for the fishes by now,' said Japheth.

'Father will be livid!' they said.

At that moment Noah's brother staggered out of one of the hatchways. Shem, Ham and Japheth heaved a great sigh of relief, not because their uncle's life had been spared, but because they had been spared their father's wrath. They turned upon Hazardikladoram as one man.

'Get below!' bawled Shem. 'Make sure there are no leaks!'

'And while you're about it,' shouted Ham, 'you can feed the animals!'

'You can muck 'em out too!' bellowed Japheth.

Wearily, Yessah went below again. All night, while the family slept, he worked at the tasks his nephews had set him. By the time he had finished he was aching all over, filthy dirty and very hungry.

It was broad daylight again when at last he made his way to the galley. Perhaps, he thought, there'll

be a nice hot bowl of vegetable soup for me. I'm
starving.

But when he got there, Mrs Noah came out.

'Hey you!' she said, 'take this,' and she thrust a
big plate of roast beef at him.

'It's meat,' said Yessah. 'I can't eat that.'

Mrs Noah looked at him disgustedly.

'I should jolly well think you can't,' she said. 'It's for Noah. Hurry up and take it to him, he's had a long, hard night.'

'Dirty, lazy old thing,' she said to her three daughters-in-law when Yessah had gone, 'he's no better than an animal. Why he had to be saved from the Flood, God alone knows.'

Chapter Four

In truth, if Yessah was no better than the animals, he could have been proud of the fact; for they could not have been more kindly and thoughtful.

Once they realized what a state the old man was in, they all wanted to help. Noah and the rest, they knew, killed animals for food, but Noah's brother had never hurt a flea. They got together to see what they could do.

The first thing Yessah needed, they decided, was food. This turned out to be an easy matter. One of the pair of buffaloes had lost her calf just before being chosen to go aboard the Ark, and she told Yessah she would be only too pleased to be milked. Next, there were plenty of eggs: a lot of hen birds had already begun to lay, and Yessah was able to choose from many different sorts. As for vegetables and fruit, these were kept in Mrs Noah's store; but when her back was turned, two furry little grey

shapes popped in, and out again, with a bunch of grapes and a handful of radishes. The monkeys were quick and careful, and Mrs Noah never noticed them.

So, at last, Yessah sat down to eat a splendid breakfast, deep in the lowest, darkest part of the belly of the Ark.

He drank thirstily from a great pitcher of warm buffalo milk, and chewed hungrily on the radishes. Then he swallowed the grapes whole, pips and all.

Finally he ate a raw egg. Which may not sound much, but it was an ostrich's egg.

'Lovely!' he said, rubbing his tummy. 'Now I simply must sleep. I can't keep my eyes open.'

'Not yet, Yessah,' said the bull elephant, 'first, a bath.' He stuck his trunk out of a port-hole and sucked, then squirted a great jet of water over Yessah, again and again, till all the dirt and filth was washed away. Now Yessah stood clean but shivering in his soaking-wet clothes.

'We'll soon warm you up,' said one of the grizzly bears, and she took the little man in her arms, hugging him very carefully against her hot, hairy chest until he was as dry as a bone.

'Now you can sleep, Master,' cooed Peace and Goodwill, and Yessah saw that the most comfortable bed you can imagine had been made for him.

For a mattress, there were two great tigers, lying back to back; Yessah stretched himself between them, upon the striped velvet of their glowing hides. He rested his weary head on a pillow of warm, furry wolfskin (with a wolf inside it). Just as he was dropping off to sleep, he felt as though the lightest, softest coverlet had been pulled over him to keep him cosy, for down fluttered a blanket of little birds – finches, robins, wrens and many more, one pair of each – and they settled gently upon Noah's brother, spreading their small wings over him.

Throughout that day Yessah slept. Three times Noah sent his sons in turn, to see that all was well below decks, first Shem, then Ham, and lastly Japheth; but each had difficulty in carrying out the order.

Shem fell flat on his face on the upper deck when something that hissed wound itself round his ankles. Ham, on the middle deck, had a sharp disagreement with a porcupine. Japheth went furthest, actually beginning to climb down the ladder that led to the lowest deck, when suddenly he heard a deep, rumbling sound, and looked down to see a lion's mouth underneath him, wide open.

However, each son told his father that all was well, and Yessah slept soundly on his luxurious bed, warm and dry.

High above him, Noah stood gazing across the waste of waters while the never-ending rain ran down the slopes of his great craggy face and dripped from the cliff of his beard.

He was not thinking of his wife, or of his sons and their wives, or the animals, or the Ark itself. He was thinking about his brother.

Noah did not doubt, for he had great faith, that one day the Flood would subside and the Ark would come to rest on dry land. Then all the creatures would be let go, to breed and fill the empty land with their offspring. Noah's sons would found great families of their own to form a mighty tribe of men with Noah himself at the head of it, Mrs Noah by his side. All that was fine, and just as it should be, but what about that scrawny old brother of his? He had no wife, no children; he would be of no use in the brave new world ahead. Just an extra mouth to feed, thought Noah, and a fussy one at that. Vegetarian indeed!

'He's useful to me at present, so I'll put up with him till the end of the voyage,' growled Noah, and the thunder growled back at him. 'But once the animals are gone, he'll have to go too, for good. No need for future generations to know that the great Noah ever had a brother!'

Chapter Five

It is an interesting fact (which few people know) that the Ark was at one time in danger of sinking. If that had happened, of course, not even a few people would have known about it. No one would have known, because Noah's family would have drowned and left a world empty of human beings for evermore.

Luckily there was one man aboard the Ark who saved it from going down. It wasn't Shem, or Ham, or Japheth, or even Noah himself: it was Noah's brother.

It happened when the Ark had been afloat for three weeks. Noah had just taken out his knife and cut the twenty-first notch in the back of Mrs Noah's neck. It wasn't the real Mrs Noah, but a wooden figure-head carved to look like her and fixed to the prow of the boat. Yessah had made it when they

were building the Ark. He was brilliant at carving things like animals from wood, so Noah told him to make a likeness of his wife. Mrs Noah was not especially good-looking so Yessah was careful to make the carving flattering, giving her a fine curved nose and large eyes to gaze out over the limitless expanse of water.

However, once the Ark was afloat, no one could see the face of the figure-head. They would have been surprised at the change in it. One day early in the voyage, when Mrs Noah had been especially bossy to Yessah, shouting, 'Hey you! Do this,' and 'Hey you! Do that,' all morning, he had decided to get his own back. He waited till no one was looking, and then he climbed out on to the figure-head. With a few deft cuts he altered its appearance.

Little did Noah know, as he made the twenty-first notch, that Mrs Noah's nose was now an ugly blob and her eyes were horribly crossed. Little did he know either, that day or indeed ever, what was happening on the lowest deck.

Nobody had noticed that over those first three weeks the Ark had been gradually settling lower and lower in the water. It hadn't sprung any leaks, for the pitch had kept its hull quite watertight, and it hadn't run against any rocks, for even the tops of the mountains were far below. What had happened, quite simply, was this: twenty-one days and nights of non-stop, pouring rain had made every plank of its gopher-wood timbers soggy, soaking and waterlogged. The Ark was sinking under its own weight.

Yessah was busy on the lowest deck, and the first he knew of it was when water began dribbling over the edge of the port-holes. (There were six port-holes at this level, three to a side. A cubit is the length from a man's elbow to the end of his middle finger, and when the Ark first floated, each port-hole was 4 cubits above the water-level.) Now, as Yessah poked his head out, he found to his horror that the surface of the Flood was just under his nose. Once it began to pour in, the Ark would settle deeper and deeper till, at last, it sank like a stone.

There wasn't a moment to lose: the port-holes must be blocked. But how? There was only one way to block them, Yessah realized – with animals; but if he asked the animals to stick their heads through the holes, they would drown. Their bottoms, then. Yes! That was it! The port-holes must be blocked by bottoms – the biggest bottoms he could find!

Within minutes Yessah had the situation under control. He called up the two elephants, the two hippos, and the two rhinos, and backed them up

against the port-holes. Each animal faced its mate on the opposite side, and so the boat was kept on an even keel. Not a drop of water came in.

To relieve them, Yessah formed a team of six bears: two polar, two black and two grizzly. Their bottoms were not as big, and, when they took their turn, some water did seep in but the elephants soon pumped it out again.

And so, you see, mankind was saved by the quick thinking of one little old bald-headed man.

By the time Noah had cut his twenty-eighth notch in Mrs Noah's neck, the danger (of which he knew nothing) was mostly over. The gopher wood had soaked up all the water it could, and the Ark rode no lower. Certainly it sailed very slowly and sluggishly but that didn't matter: it wasn't going anywhere special.

So the days passed, with no sign of any change in the weather. The rain fell relentlessly upon the dark waters that covered the earth. Yessah worked hard looking after the animals, and the animals in their turn looked after him.

Every day they made sure he was well fed. The cow buffalo gave plenty of rich milk, the monkeys stole all sorts of fruit and vegetables from the store; and as for eggs, Yessah had the choice of hundreds of different kinds. Every night his lovely warm, living bed was ready for him.

Up in the galley, Mrs Noah and her daughters-in-law worked hard too, cooking great meals of meat for their men on a stove that was always in danger of going out in all that wet. Mrs Noah grew more and more crusty, shouting 'Hey you!' at Yessah whenever she caught sight of him (which he made sure was as seldom as possible).

On the upper deck, Shem, Ham and Japheth worked sulkily, looking after the small creatures that lived up there: little snakes, frogs, lizards and various beetles; they did not venture down into either of the lower decks any more and so were always soaking wet.

Wettest of all was Noah on the poop-deck, watching always for some sign of the end of the Flood.

Increasingly he longed for the moment when the Ark should settle on dry land and he could be rid

of his bleating, lowing, roaring, barking, squawk-
ing, smelly cargo, and especially that useless old
brother of his.

On the morning he cut his fortieth notch on the
figure-head, he decided to act.

'Send for my brother!' he bellowed down to Mrs
Noah, and she in turn yelled down to Yessah.

'Hey you!' she hollered. 'Noah wants you!'

Hastily Noah's brother swallowed the last
mouthful of a delicious omelette made from pea-
cocks' and pheasants' eggs, and climbed to the
poop-deck.

'Yessah?' he said.

'Fetch me a bird, Brother,' said Noah, 'I want
to send one out to see if there's any sign of dry
land.'

So Yessah fetched one of the ravens, which flew
till it was out of sight. They waited, but it never
returned.

'Fetch another,' said Noah angrily; and then a
thought struck him.

'Fetch a dove,' he said.

Yessah went weak at the knees. Oh, not my dear

Peace or my dear Goodwill, he thought frantically,
I couldn't bear to lose one of them.

'A turtle-dove, Noah?' he said in a pleading
voice. 'Or a rock-dove?'

'No,' said Noah. 'One of your precious white
ones.'

Chapter Six

Down in the lowest, darkest part of the belly of the Ark, the elephants had just finished their first task of the day, pumping water out, when Yessah climbed down the ladder. Even in the semi-darkness they could see his face was white, as white as his two friends who came fluttering to perch on his thin shoulders.

'Why, whatever is the matter, best of men?' trumpeted the cow elephant, and at the sound of her voice the other beasts gathered round. Only the hen raven sat black and silent upon her perch.

'What is it, Master?' asked Peace and Goodwill.

'The raven,' said Yessah slowly. 'He has not returned. Now Noah wants one of you, my dears, to fly out and look for land.'

'Ah!' breathed the listening crowd, for they knew how much the doves meant to Noah's brother.

'What Noah wants is one thing,' said Peace.

'But what you want is another,' said Goodwill

'Do *you* want one of us to go, Master?' they said.

Yessah hesitated.

'Oh dear!' he cried miserably. 'I could not *order* either of you to undertake so dangerous a task Even if you found the dry land for which we al long, you might never find your way back to the Ark again. I might never see you again.'

'Nevermore!' croaked the hen raven.

For a moment all the animals were silent, and then 'Rubbish!' said Peace in a cheery voice. 'Of course you will see me again, Master.'

'Wait! Why you? Let me go!' cried Goodwill to his mate, but, before he could make a move, she flew out of the nearest port-hole.

Yessah spent the rest of the day in an agony of suspense. He could not keep his mind on his work for worrying about Peace; he fed hay to the lions and tigers, and gave the giraffes a huge bone each, much to their surprise.

In the afternoon he was summoned to the

poop-deck, where he found Noah with a very tired-looking white dove upon his wrist. Yessah took Peace below, and dried and warmed her, then Goodwill brought food to his mate and popped it into her gaping beak as though she were a nestling chick.

'Nothing,' she said, when at last she was rested. 'There was nothing but water and yet more water. The world is one enormous sea.'

Yessah spent the next few days worrying that Peace might be sent out again, and just when he had begun to relax a little and forget about it, she was.

There were forty-seven notches on the neck of the figure-head when, at Noah's orders, Peace flew away once more.

'Try not to worry, my dear,' said Yessah to Goodwill, smoothing his feathers. 'She'll come back, I'm sure,' and she did, just before sundown. But this time she carried something in her beak.

Everyone came running at Noah's great shout.

'Behold!' he cried to the family.

And they beheld.

'It's a dove,' said Ham, who wasn't very bright. Japheth and Shem were not much better.

'It's got something in its beak,' said one.

'Looks like a twig with leaves on it,' said the other.

Mrs Noah was the best of a bad bunch. She was after all a cook, and cooks used oil, and oil came from olives.

'It's an olive twig,' she said.

'Of course it's an olive twig!' roared Noah. 'Any fool can see that. But where did it come from?'

'Off an olive tree?' said Ham hopefully.

'Well, what does that mean, you dolt?' shouted Noah. 'Can none of you see what it means?'

His brick-red face turned purple.

'Begone!' he bellowed at the family.

And they bewent.

Only Yessah stood his ground, though he was shaking with fear at his brother's anger.

'Well?' shouted Noah.

'It m-means that the Flood is beginning to go down. Somewhere, there is a tree sticking up above the water.'

'You're not as stupid as you look,' said Noah

'P-please,' said Yessah, 'can I have my dov[e]
back?'

'Take your bird,' growled Noah, 'but I sha[ll]
want it again, one week from today.'

There was great excitement as news of the oliv[e]
twig spread round the boat, the boat in which the[y]
had all been confined for so long, cramped, damp

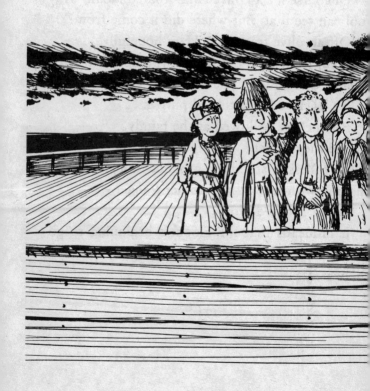

and often sea-sick. All the animals were indeed
heartily sick of the sea and longing to stretch their
legs, or their wings, or their coils once again.

'How we will run!' cried the gazelles.

'How we will soar!' cried the eagles.

'How we will hop!' cried the kangaroos.

'How we will climb!' cried the monkeys.

'How we will eat ants!' cried the anteaters.

The ants just cried.

Seven more days passed; Noah cut the fifty-fourth notch in the back of Mrs Noah's neck, and away went Peace for the third time.

Noah's brother watched until she disappeared from sight. He held Goodwill gently in his hands.

'Don't worry, my dear,' he said once again. 'She will come back.'

They watched and they waited, they waited and they watched, that day and for many days, for the dove called Peace to return to the Ark. But she did not return.

Chapter Seven

Yessah was very unhappy at the loss of Peace, and it did not help to hear the sad voice of Goodwill mourning softly for his mate. But then one day something happened that shook both of them out of their misery. In fact it shook everyone aboard. Suddenly, with a crash, the Ark ran aground!

At the impact, Yessah thought they had hit a whale. He rushed to the nearest port-hole and saw, to his amazement, a wall of rock. It was the same on the other side of the boat. He ran up on to the upper deck.

The boat was held firmly in the trough of a V-shaped outcrop, on the top of what seemed to be a small island. But as the family watched, they saw the water level receding like an outgoing tide. The Ark was in fact stuck, high and dry, on top of a mountain.

There did not appear to be much damage, except to the figure-head; Mrs Noah's face, Yessah was not sorry to see, had taken a bashing. They all turned to look at Noah standing up above them on the poop-deck.

'Where are we, Father?' shouted Shem.

Noah stood tall, feet firmly planted on the deck that would never move beneath him again. He threw wide his arms and raised his great bearded face to the heavens, and, after a quick peep down to make sure they were all watching, cried in ringing tones, 'Oh, people of Noah! We are upon a mountain!'

'What's it called, Father?' shouted Japheth.

Noah hesitated. He hadn't a clue, but it would never do for the all-knowing Noah to admit this. Then he had a piece of luck: when the boat had struck the rock, the two rats on board had reacted as rats always do.

'It's a sinking ship!' cried one.

'Then we'll leave it!' cried the other.

Now they ran across the upper deck on their

way to leap over the side in such haste that one o
them scuttled across Mrs Noah's feet, just afte
Japheth had asked his question.

'It . . . is . . . called . . .' began Noah slowly and
at that instant, Mrs Noah yelled, 'Ar! A rat!'

Ham grinned his rather foolish grin.

'Father!' he shouted. 'Mother says it's calle
Ararat.'

'She took the word right out of my mouth,' sai
Noah. 'We are indeed, as I was about to tell you
upon the summit of Mount Ararat. Let down th
gangway!'

And Shem, Ham and Japheth let it down.

It is an interesting fact (which few people know
that Noah did not allow all the animals to g
after the Flood. Oh no. He was not so silly. H
knew that farming would be the only life for hi
family, and that their first task was to begin th
breeding of flocks and herds to feed the grea
tribe, as yet unborn, of which he would be th
head.

So he ordered his sons to keep back the buffaloes, the sheep and the goats; and animals to provide stock for riding upon, or for pulling ploughs and carts, like the donkeys and the camels; and many other kinds of beasts and birds that a farmer would need. By nightfall, these were the only creatures left in the Ark. The rest were gone. The birds had flown, except for two, one white and one black, that had no mate; the animals had marched (and hopped, and crawled, and wriggled), two by two down the gangway, down the mountainside, away into the drying world.

The next morning Noah called a family conference on the poop-deck, but first he needed Yessah out of the way. He sent for his brother.

'Brother,' he said, 'go down to the bottom of Mount Ararat and have a good look at the lie of the land. Go to the west, then come back and tell me. No hurry.'

'Yessah,' said Noah's brother.

Noah watched the thin, bald-headed figure

picking his way down the slopes, and then turne[d]
to the others.

'My brother,' he said, 'has gone west. He wi[ll]
not be back for some while.'

Mrs Noah sniffed. 'Pity he has to come back a[t] all,' she said, 'he's only going to be a burden to u[s] when we set out.'

Noah looked at the others.

'Is that the feeling of you all?' he said.

Shem, Ham, Japheth and their wives nodde[d] their heads vigorously.

'We don't want him tagging along with us[,] Father,' said Shem.

'Just another mouth to feed,' said Japheth.

'On cabbages,' said Ham, grinning, 'like an ol[d] rabbit.'

'You are speaking,' said Noah severely, 'o[f] Hazardikladoram, brother of Noah.'

'No one need ever know, Noah,' said Mrs Noah[.] 'When they come to tell the history of the grea[t] Noah, no one need ever know that he had [a] brother.'

'How then shall we be rid of him?' said Noah[.] He suspected that Ham or his brothers woul[d] cheerfully have wrung the old rabbit's neck, but h[e] did not want to be the one to suggest it.

'Easy,' said Mrs Noah. 'He can have this filthy old Ark to himself. He's a vegetarian; he can finish up the hay. Let us take the rest of the animals and go; he's gone west, we'll go east. Now – fast!'

She took a sly look at her husband.

'If Noah so decrees,' she added.

Noah gave a fine imitation of a man forced, much against his will, to leave his only brother. He stared sadly westward, smote himself upon the brow and let out a long shuddering sigh.

'I so decree,' he said at last in a hollow voice, and off the others hurried to get things ready.

Noah climbed down from the poop-deck and walked forward to the prow of the boat to the disfigured figure-head. He patted the top of Mrs Noah's gopher-wood head.

'You took the words right out of my mouth,' he said. 'One day, men will write in a great book about the beginnings of the world. Noah's name will be written large, and the story of Noah's Ark; and the names of Noah's sons and their sons and

their sons' sons that shall found all the nations of the earth. But nowhere in its pages will you find the name of Hazardikladoram.'

He was right. You won't.

Chapter Eight

When Yessah reached the bottom of the mountain, he found everything looking pretty strange. The Flood had gone down miraculously, but still there were great pools and lakes everywhere. The trees appeared limp and soggy, like giant seaweeds, from being under water for such a time.

But already the world looked so much better. The golden sun was shining again, the sky was blue. As Yessah looked up into it he saw, high above, a large black bird gliding and wheeling as though it were searching for something below. When it saw Yessah, it shut its wings and dived towards him. It was the male raven that Noah had sent out on the fortieth day.

'Am I glad to see you!' croaked the bird, as it landed and hopped up to Noah's brother. 'I searched the world for that beastly boat and couldn't find it. I've been away ages. My mate will

be raven mad. Where is she?'

Yessah pointed to the summit.

'Before you go,' he said, 'tell me. Have you seen any sign of my white dove, Peace?'

'Afraid not,' said the raven. 'I only saw seabirds and waterfowl. Sorry!' And he flapped away up the western slopes of Mount Ararat.

Yessah explored the plain at the mountain's foot for some time, and then he set off to return to the Ark.

It was long past midday when at last he neared it, though the stable smell of it came to him on the wind some while before. Smell and noise, thought Yessah, that's what I shall always remember about the voyage, especially noise. Twenty-four-hour noise it was: first from the creatures of the day and then from those of the night, and from Noah bawling orders and Mrs Noah yelling 'Hey you!' Funny, it seems strangely quiet now.

Yessah climbed the gangway and went aft to the poop-deck.

'Noah!' he called, but there was no reply.

He searched the upper deck. There was no sign of his three nephews, and no animals.

On the middle deck, the galley was empty, the stove cold, and again all the beasts were gone. He looked in Mrs Noah's store to see what was left, but there was only one wrinkled apple.

It was the same on his own deck, the bottom deck – the lowest, darkest part of the belly of the Ark. There was not a single creature to be seen. Where's Goodwill, thought Yessah, surely he has not left me?

Once again he searched the boat calling, 'Goodwill! Goodwill! Where are you, my dear? Come to old Yessah,' but there was no answer.

There was no sound to be heard but the sigh of the wind as Noah's brother sat eating a mouldy apple in an empty boat on top of a lonely mountain.

Just for a moment Yessah felt very sorry for himself, but he was a tough old man, and he had had 708 years to learn one of life's most useful lessons. Whenever you feel really depressed, count your blessings. Yessah counted his.

First, he was alive, which he would not have been if his brother had not ordered the building of the Ark, nor indeed if the python had not rescued him at the start of the Flood, or if the other animals had not nursed and tended him.

Which led him to count his second blessing, the company of the animals. He would never be lonely wherever he went, even though now he had no family.

This led him to count his third blessing, that now he had no family.

At that moment he knew for certain that he wasn't going to miss any of them for one second, ever again. There were only two living things in the world that he was missing, terribly. He could only hope that Goodwill might find his mate, Peace, once more.

Thinking about the doves made Yessah look up into the heavens and he noticed what a beautiful evening it was, warm and sunny. And, as he looked,

he saw to his amazement a great arch of colour beginning to form in the sky.

Far away to the east, where a little last rain was still falling, Noah and his party saw it too as they drove their beasts onward. It curved down from

the heavens and seemed to plunge into the ground just ahead of them. They pressed on, hoping to reach the end of it, yet it always eluded them.

But the western end of the great, glowing arch fell full upon Yessah, as he sat in the empty Ark and marvelled. He had never seen such a thing before. There had never been such a thing before.

Seven brilliant colours shone down upon him – red, orange, yellow, green, blue, indigo and violet – and then suddenly an eighth was added, as two snow-white shapes came winging down the curve of the rainbow and settled upon the thin shoulders of Noah's brother. 'Peace,' said one softly in his left ear, and 'Goodwill,' said the other in his right.

It is an interesting fact (which everybody knows) that the children of Noah fathered all the nations of the earth; nations that to this day quarrel with each other, fight with each other, torture and starve and kill each other, with a greed and cruelty that not one of the animals in the Ark would possibly have understood.

Everybody knows that.

But do you know what happened to Noah's
brother? I'll tell you.

With Peace and Goodwill, he lived happily.

Ever after.

Some other titles available in Puffin

THE MOUSE AND HIS CHILD
Russell Hoban

From the safety of the toyshop to slavery in the dump and escape through wood and meadow; through war between armies of shrews, through a first-night disaster with Crow's travelling players, through Muskrat's horrendous exercise in pure science and an encounter with a deep-thinking snapping turtle and the Last Visible Dog at the bottom of a pond; all the way to the final battle for their territory, the clockwork mouse and his child endure whatever comes their way in their quest for the beautiful dolls' house they once had known.

THE HOUNDS OF THE MORRIGAN
Pat O'Shea

Whoever would have thought that the old manuscript in the bookshop would have led them into the journey of a lifetime? This was no fairy story; it was a real quest of good versus evil in which Pidge and his sister Brigit were the crusaders. The journey began in Ireland with the destination unknown. Time became meaningless, magic was everywhere. But always at their backs they could feel the terrible hounds of the Morrigan looking to their mistress for the signal to attack . . .

JELLYBEAN
Tessa Duder

A sensitive modern novel about Geraldine, alias 'Jellybean', who leads a rather solitary life as the only child of a single parent. She's tired of having to fit in with her mother's busy schedule, but a new friend and a performance of 'The Nutcracker Suite' change everything.

THE PRIESTS OF FERRIS
Maurice Gee

Susan Ferris and her cousin Nick return to the world of O which they had saved from the evil Halfmen, only to find that O is not ruled by cruel and ruthless priests. Can they save the inhabitants of O from tyranny? An action-packed and gripping story by the author of prize-winning *The Halfmen of O*.

MAN IN MOTION
Jan Mark

Once Lloyd has started at his new school, he soon finds he's playing cricket with Salman, swimming with Kenneth, cycling with James and playing badminton with Vlad. But American football is Lloyd's greatest enthusiasm. And in time it tests his loyalties, not only to his other sporting activities, but also to the new friends he shares them with.

THE OUTSIDE CHILD
Nina Bawden

Imagine suddenly discovering you have a step-brother and -sister no one has ever told you about? It's the most exciting thing that's ever happened to Jane, and she can't wait to meet them. Perhaps at last she will become part of a 'proper' family, instead of forever being the outside child. So begins a long search for her brother and sister, but when she finally does track them down, Jane finds there are still more surprises in store!

THE SEA IS SINGING

Rosalind Kerven

In her seaside Shetland home, Tess is torn between the plight of
the whales and loyalty to her father and his job on the oil rig. A
haunting and though-provoking novel.

BACK HOME

Michelle Magorian

A marvellously gripping story of an irrepressible girl's struggle
to adjust to a new life. Twelve-year-old Rusty, who had been
evacuated to the United States when she was seven, returns to
the grey austerity of post-war Britain.

THE FOX OF SKELLAND
Rachel Dixon

Samantha's never liked the old custom of Foxing Day – the fox costume especially gives her the creeps. So when Jason and Rib, children of the new publicans at The Fox and Lady, find the costume and Jason wears it to the fancy-dress disco, she's sure something awful will happen. Then Sam's old friend Joseph sees the ghost of the Lady and her fox. Has she really come back to exact vengeance on the village? Or has her appearance got something to do with the spate of burglaries in the area?

MARIANNE DREAMS
Catherine Storr

Soon after Marianne found the pencil in the old workbox, she began to have strange dreams of an old house, with a boy in the upstairs room. Then the amazing truth dawned on her: it was *she* who had created the house and the boy because whenever she drew something during the day, that night she would dream about it. As the dreams become more sinister, and it seems that the boy is in great danger, so Marianne wonders whether she is to be trapped forever in a cycle of pictures and dreams . . .